PERFECT

BEAUTIFUL ORDINARY
BOOK 2

S.A. MCEWEN

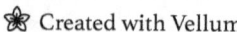

PERFECT

BEAUTIFUL ORDINARY
BOOK 2

S.A. MCEWEN

ALSO BY THE AUTHOR

Romantic Suspense

Close (Beautiful Ordinary #1)

Ruined (Beautiful Ordinary Book 3)

Domestic Thrillers

The Good Daughter

The Lost Boy

Good Girl Bad

Sister in Trouble

Please Note: *Ruined* and *The Good Daughter* are a steamy and non-steamy version of the same book

To my husband, who supports even my wackiest, most outrageous ideas—
Your belief in me is the steadiest, most comforting thing in the entire world.

PROLOGUE

Ada

October 24, 2015

Waves lap gently at the hull of the boat.

The sky through the small window beside the bed is almost black.

Two champagne glasses on the tiny bedside table list and clink gently with the swell.

The naked man on the bed lets out a long sigh.

He's too drunk to take in the flawlessness of the scene.

The scene that—even by my exacting standards, even on short notice—is utterly perfect.

On the surface.

If you ignore a few crucial underlying details.

But I push them out of my mind, gather my things, scurry onto the pier, and walk away.

I stumble on the uneven surface—the finality of the moment marred by my awkwardness in my impractical heels.

But I leave. That's the important thing.

That should have been where our story ends.

Perhaps I should have slapped him.

Stabbed him, even.

Because then the story really would have ended there.

But stories don't always end the way you want them to.

1

ADA

Two years later—November 11, 2017

"Well. This is awkward."

Ben turns toward me, blue eyes twinkling, amusement oozing out of every damn perfect inch of him. He's lounging backwards, one well-defined bicep tantalisingly close, hanging over the back of the stiff-backed chair as he turns toward me.

The man is imperturbable.

"I can't believe that being seated together at a wedding is the thing that springs to mind as 'awkward' for you," he murmurs. "I could think of a few more blush-worthy examples."

He watches me beneath his ridiculously long black eyelashes, the corners of his mouth curling slightly in the hint of a smile.

"We agreed not to see each other anymore. So, yes, this is awkward, if you ask me." I observe him with a blank expression, tilting my head slightly to the side, as though mildly disinterested in his failure to understand. An expression that I know for a fact he finds equally as intoxicating as I find the amused grin he is throwing my way.

It pitches his competitive streak into overdrive.

He always wants to plant some emotion on my blank

expression. Overlay it with something more spontaneous. Something that offers a crack into my soul.

His lips curl slightly more, and he leans in toward me, the smell of his aftershave enough to make me inhale sharply. I want to close my eyes—partly to lose myself in it, but also to gather some resolve to fight the swell of longing it induces. But I hold my expression, the angle of my head, and watch him innocently.

It's hard to stop the games with Ben, whatever we've agreed to.

Whatever I know is for the best.

"As I recall," he drawls, deliberately letting his hand brush mine as he reaches for his champagne glass. I jump inadvertently. His skin feels more alive to me than any other texture on the planet. I feel his touch in my very core, every time.

He clocks my reaction and allows himself a tiny victory smile, his eyes telling me exactly what he's thinking: *I can win this. You know I can.* Then he continues: "We didn't agree to anything. You told me what was happening. Via SMS. Classy. Surprising, even for you."

I keep my face deadpan. I haven't actually spoken to the man since my curt text message three weeks ago, pointedly ignoring his calls. He's right—I didn't give him any right of reply. But it's not like we haven't discussed this before.

"It was time," I reply, my voice calm and cool, betraying nothing of the feelings underneath it. The uncertainty, the desire. The regret. "You knew it was coming. It's been fun. But let's leave it at that."

"*Funnnnn,*" Ben repeats, his parted lips lingering on the *n,* watching me with an unreadable expression. "That's not the word that I'd have used to describe it."

"Really? What would you choose?"

I can't help myself; I want to know what word he'd choose. What word he'd wrap around us, exult us with.

I know ending it is the right decision. I know it's all wrong,

Ben and I. But my heart still soars at the possibilities this unknown word choice offers. Like one right word could melt my heart.

He sips his champagne, watching me closely. He knows I'm hanging on his damn word.

That's the problem, when you know each other as well as we do. When you've known each other for most of your lives. There's no hiding. He can see me like I can't even see myself.

"One word?" he asks, stalling, his eyes fast on mine, his long fingers curling sensually around the stem of his delicate glass, his full lips aggressively tantalising just by their mere existence. But he presses them together slightly, nonetheless, watching me watching them.

He smooths his napkin, dragging this out, his face a mask— but I know exactly what he's feeling.

Satisfaction, at me hanging on his every word.

Hurt, that I put an end to us.

Longing. Hoping to seduce me with his eyes, his mouth, his fingers. Hoping that I'll change my mind.

Hope: that's always the killer for me. Ben, with his huge, hopeful eyes, full of all the feelings.

He looks back up at me, a deliberate blink, his eyes dark and brooding, saying all the things I love to see. How much he wants me. How well he knows me. How the whole world stops and slows when we're together. It's like being on some kind of slow-motion fair ride. Or maybe a movie trailer with special effects: bright lights, seductive music—the whole nine yards. Just us, in the middle. Everything else fading to a blur around us, a dull roar of inconsequential sound and colour. Where the only thing that matters is us.

In this space with him, I feel my most alive.

He speaks slowly, intentionally. Unflustered as ever. And as he speaks, he lets one hand drop under the tablecloth, sliding it up the inside of my leg, slowly, provocatively. Dangerously.

His fingers are light, brushing against me, his touch so familiar: warm and masculine and possessive and promising. His eyes don't leave mine, and he leans in even closer, his next words a caress against my cheek, the corner of my lips.

"If I only had one word?" he says, "I'd choose...*perfect*."

I inhale sharply, at his fingers as much as his word, though both are exhilarating. One hand automatically flies to his arm, my fingers curling around his bicep, the gesture at once both intimate and grounding.

My rock.

My one true love.

His eyes continue to hold mine, languid, satisfied.

Ben 1, Ada 0, they say.

Then he withdraws his hand, downs his champagne, raises his eyebrows at me, and stands up and walks away.

2

BEN

"Chloe." I try to keep my voice light, but a fool could hear the resignation in it.

"Ben," she replies brightly, her social cheer grating after only one damn word. "Enjoying the wedding? Such a gorgeous bride! Spectacular dress. Those shoes! Makes you all woozy, doesn't it?"

There's no point trying to clarify—a conversation with Chloe is like being caught in a tornado. None of it makes any sense or is at a pace you can decipher until the punch she's been trying to camouflage under all her niceties hits you in the face, full force.

It's an attack by sheer confusion.

"So nice to see the family! Everyone together—happens so rarely these days. Your dad looks very fine. Did you help him pick the suit? No, of course not. He's a grown man, no help required!" Her sentences run together, falsely bright, with an undercurrent of agitation. I've learnt to just wait for the point, not get sidetracked by the reams of spewing chatter.

"God, how many of these have we been to over the last few years? I'm sure it will be your turn soon! Seeing anyone special at the moment? So hard to meet people these days, isn't it? Thank

God I met Trevor before all this godawful Tinder and Twitter and internet dating! Just a regular old meeting for us!"

I watch Chloe with a kind of scientific interest. She's actually an incredibly successful woman. It's hard to pick exactly what her high-speed interactions are all about. She surely could not be this scattered and wired in managerial meetings? It strikes me, once again, as almost adolescent in its nerviness.

Being Ada's sister, and someone I ideally want on my side, she is someone I usually humour. But today, I feel pissed.

"Is there something you want to discuss, Chloe?" I ask her pointedly. "I was on my way to get a top up." I hold up my empty champagne glass and wiggle it for effect, highlighting the importance of my errand. Doubly important now. If she wants to chat, I need a bloody drink in hand.

Her eyes fasten on mine, stern and piercing. "Yes, actually," she says, her voice suddenly evening out. Sounding adult and firm. Like she might dictate some terms and expects, through years of experience, for the recipient to listen.

Ah, I think to myself. *There's a manager I can better imagine.*

"Now that you mention it," she adds, as though her next sentence is an afterthought. As though it wouldn't have come out without my prompting.

"It's about Ada," she goes on, her eyes like a vice against my own. She's not going to let this go, whatever it is, without something from me. Inwardly, I sigh deeply.

Chloe knows about my history with Ada. She doesn't like it, but she's never said a word about it directly. She frowns at me occasionally, but that's the extent of our interactions on the subject.

So I wait with interest to see what she's going to say now.

"It's about Kingston." She watches me carefully.

That stops me short.

"What about him?" I ask equally carefully, my face deliberately blank.

Kingston is the last reason Ada called off our...*thing,* a few years back.

Last reason before now, I correct myself.

Then I frown, irritated that I can't think of a better word to describe us. Our relationship? Affair? Neither one is quite right.

Chloe continues to watch me. She seems on edge. Sharp. Less fluttery and full of nonsense. It's so unusual that my tendency to dismiss her is sidelined. Something is up, and my focus sharpens too. So I wait, giving nothing away.

I'm not afraid of what Chloe thinks of Ada and me, but I don't want her to know how little information I have about the competition.

Chloe speaks slowly, searching my face.

"She got another letter."

BACK NEXT TO Ada for the speeches, I drum my fingers on the white linen tablecloth impatiently.

She elbows me discreetly, frowning.

"Shhhh," she hisses. But I can barely wait for everyone to shut up so I can turn my attention to more important conversations. Eventually I hiss back, "We need to talk. Now."

She stares rigidly ahead, not giving me any eye contact, pointedly smiling and nodding at Aunty Kate's longwinded rendition of how the happy couple met. Her speech is laced with relief that her eldest daughter finally, *finally* (age 43) found someone, though of course she doesn't say anything of the sort.

You don't have to say everything out loud in families. Sometimes everyone knows it all, all too well.

Usually I'd be in my element. Champagne, family, laughter, dancing. A cousin's wedding—sitting next to Ada—would be high up on my list of enjoyable ways to spend a Saturday. But between the breakup via SMS and Kingston's letter, I'm not in the mood for fun or romance anymore.

Finally the speeches are over. But when I turn to Ada, she's pointing to the dance floor. The newlyweds are standing awkwardly alone up there. The band are still fiddling with strings and microphones and appear to be in no hurry to start the music. And neither bride nor groom is comfortable in the spotlight. Everyone is facing toward them, waiting for their first dance. They look absolutely petrified.

Without thinking, I stand. Raise my champagne glass. The guests cheer loudly; they're all half-cut already. I barely have to say anything—propose a toast, talk about that time I first met Kate, some admirable quality she displayed. An anecdote that highlights her cheerfulness, her thoughtfulness. Unconsciously, I compare her to myself in that instance, self-deprecating and silly. The crowd laughs appreciatively. They all know me so well anyway.

I sit down when the lead singer coughs into the mike.

When I turn back to Ada, she looks warmer. She smiles at me with genuine affection. She's grateful for my intervention, and I pounce on the advantage it affords me without missing a beat.

"Ada. Chloe tells me there's a problem with Kingston. Tell me about these letters she's so worked up over."

For the briefest second, I see something I'd call fear pass across her face. But it is immediately replaced by a frown, a flash of anger. Her whole body stiffens.

"That's not any of your business. And Chloe had no right talking to you about it, either."

"She seems worried about you," I counter. "We both know I'm not her favourite person in the world. So if she's reaching out to me, it makes me think maybe I should be worried, too."

Ada remains stiff and on guard.

"She's overreacting, as usual." There's a hint of scorn in her voice. "Kingston wants to be 'friends.' There is no chance, ever, of that happening. Zilch. So both of you can leave it alone."

"Is he why you broke it off with me?"

She looks startled.

"Don't be stupid. You know why I broke it off. This can't go anywhere. We both just need to get on with our own lives. The longer we drag it out, the harder it will be."

I study her for a moment. Her coldness—aloofness, even—is so at odds with her appearance. Her fiery auburn hair is beautifully styled, the long tresses falling across her shoulders just so, bouncing off her glorious breasts in perfect loose curls. But even with the most careful styling in the world, her hair hints at something wild. Or maybe I've just seen it across a pillow too many times. The fullness of her lips, the shape of her eyes, the curve of her waist—she screams sensuality. Her mouth is for kissing, her body for touching. For pleasure. It's incongruous with this stiffness, this unease in her own skin.

"You're worried about something. And you broke up with me like a teenager." It's meant to be a barb, but as well as I know her, Ada knows me just as well.

She softens, squeezes my arm. "Don't worry about me. I'm fine. Let's just enjoy the party, okay? We can talk another time."

"Good. Monday. We can grab a meal after work. I'll drop by at six."

Ada opens her mouth, to protest no doubt, but our conversation is cut short in my favour. My dad and stepmother swoop in, elegant and poised. Dad claps me on the back, a little too heartily.

"Hey, kids!" he shouts, way too loud. He must have had more champagne than usual.

"Hi, Dad," I respond brightly, smiling broadly at Ada. *Ben 2, Ada 0,* my smile says. "Hi, Janey."

Ada smiles weakly. "Hi, Bill," she says. "Hi, Mum."

3

ADA

All day Monday, I curse him.

His hands, his lips.

His bloody kindheartedness and decency.

It would be much easier to break up with a psychopath.

That thought sobers me. *You did that already,* I correct myself. *And it wasn't actually very easy at all, was it?*

I pull open my top drawer and stare at the envelope inside.

Kingston.

This letter.

It makes no sense.

I'm interrupted by Tracy, an eager intern, and sigh inside. At least, I thought it was on the inside. But she stops her advance toward my desk, her eyes wide.

"Is it a bad time?" she squeaks, looking ready to flee.

"Yes," I tell her. "But you're here now. What is it?"

"Ah, I just wondered if you could help me with the formatting for the sex therapy article. I'm having trouble with the layout."

I tilt my head to the side, observing her impassively.

"You're probably best to speak to Sam or Kasey about that," I tell her. I want to shout at her that there is absolutely no possible reason for her to disturb the CEO about an everyday issue that has nothing to do with management and everything to do with design. But Jason has appeared, leaning against the doorframe and looking at me meaningfully.

After Tracy scurries away, he raises his eyebrows at me.

"Last week you were pulling her up for not running a layout past you. Today you don't want to know about it?"

"Helping format an article is different from casting a final eye over it. You know that. She ought to know that. Or someone in this office needs to teach her," I tell him crossly. "It's a waste of my time, and I have a lot to get through today."

"Hmmm," he says, pushing off the doorframe and coming closer. "You have a lot to get through every day. And that's false economy if you're going to get her to change the whole layout in the end anyway. You might as well have given input now to save everyone some time down the track."

I frown at him. It would be a whole lot more useful if Jason were as terrified of me as everybody else in the office seems to be.

"If you want to change the process, bring it up in Friday's meeting. I'm sure everybody will be delighted to hear your thoughts about it then," I say, smirking slightly, turning back to my desktop.

Jason grins at me, and I sigh again and try to focus on the article I'm reviewing. Written by my favourite freelancer, it's bright and fun and delightful. The photography is stunning. It oozes charm. It's my lead article for the month and I've been reading and rereading it all morning. The closing sentence just isn't quite right and I can't yet find an enhancement.

"Send it back to Harlow," Jason advises. "She'll come up with something. Or ask the team for input." He stands behind me and reads over my shoulder. "Or, just leave it, Ada. Jesus. It sounds great." He blows out a breath in frustration.

"You haven't even read the article," I snap at him, my eyes

glued to the screen. "It doesn't quite tie in all the themes. It's quite genius—all the threads running through this one, but they don't all wrap together at the end. I'll just go over it again and see if I can come up with something better." I wave him off in a type of dismissal, already reaching for my thesaurus and the notes I'd given Harlow prior to her interview.

"What about the team lunch? You've skived off the last five of them. You were the one who wrote all that stuff about team culture and being approachable. Jeez, some of the new staff haven't said more than hi to you."

Jason moves toward the door, but stops at the end of my desk, rapping his knuckles against it, his expression aggravated. My second-in-command of five years, he is probably the only one in the office who'll complain to me about my leadership.

"Go ahead without me," I say breezily, not looking away from my computer. I know I ought to go, but frankly, I'd rather work on this article. Partly because I can't bear the thought of a single sentence going out into the world any less than just right—but also because I prefer working to chatting.

"You mean, 'go without me,'" he corrects me, terse. "As an editor, I would think you'd be more precise with your language. Don't pretend you're going to come later."

"Okay, fine. I'm not going to come," I say, finally looking at him in irritation. "This is how I work, Jase. You know that. Stop hoping I'll change."

He sighs heavily and leaves without responding.

It's 5:30 p.m. by the time I'm happy. Although I've read the article so many times I'm not sure it even makes any sense anymore. But I've approved it for design and opened the next one.

A niggling sense of something urgent, not dealt with, keeps

troubling me though, and I remember Kingston's letter with a jolt.

I pull it out of the drawer and smooth it flat on my desk. Chloe would have a fit; she wants fingerprinting and rubber gloves. But police involvement is the last thing I want.

It's a simple typed note, only three lines long. Different to the earlier ones, which rambled for pages, nonsensical and vaguely threatening.

Threatening in their complete disconnect from reality, rather than making threats against me.

My mind flits back to our early dates. I had been desperate to move on from Ben, our pointless on-again, off-again romance. I loved him, sure. But our family would never accept us being together. So I threw myself into the first relationship I could find.

Stupid. How did I miss it? I wonder for the fifteen-hundredth time. Every other aspect of my life is attended to obsessively—pros and cons weighed, decisions agonised over—but I threw myself into that relationship like my life depended on it.

"Ada!"

My thoughts are interrupted by a shout from the reception area.

Startled, I hurriedly shove the letter back into my top drawer.

Ben pokes his head around the door as I pretend to fuss with papers on my desk. He might know about the damn letter, but I sure as hell don't want him reading it.

"Ready?" he asks, his hair flopping across his eyes, his mischievous grin clearly conveying his belief that he's winning something here.

I roll my eyes and attempt to convey right back that he's only winning because I'm letting him. I could just as easily have locked my door. But Ben's grin only widens. He's impossibly cocky and self-assured.

Sighing, I tell him that I only have an hour and slip on my shoes.

DESPITE MYSELF, it's impossible not to enjoy time spent with Ben.

He keeps up a steady stream of entertaining chatter as we wander down charming Melbourne laneways until a table takes his fancy. Perched outside on bar stools on the cobblestones, we sip wine, and everything feels just the way it always did. Even Ben's wandering, appreciative eyes don't disrupt my sense of comfort.

"Are you trying to flirt with me?" I ask, tilting my head.

"No," he shakes his head earnestly. "Absolutely not." Then he grins again. "I'm just enjoying your tits in that shirt."

I roll my eyes, and he smirks, his gaze travelling slowly downward again. Something clenches deep in my tummy.

If only he wasn't quite so sexy, damn him.

Glancing pointedly at my watch, I wonder if I should dive right in or try to distract him. But I suddenly feel exhausted. I lean forward on my elbows and close my eyes.

When I open them, Ben's expression is serious.

"Tell me about the letters."

I ponder him for a moment. If anything, I feel embarrassed.

"That guy I dated for a while. Kingston. God, even his name is stupid," I mutter, distracted, thinking that anyone who went by the nickname "King" was bound to have some issues.

"And?" Ben prompts.

"He got a bit stalker-like when I broke it off. Kept turning up. Wrote some pretty weird letters. Creeped me out that they were hand-delivered all over the place. Places he shouldn't have known I was going." I shudder, remembering.

"Jesus. Ada. Why didn't you tell me?"

"Why do you think?" I snap, irritated.

"We're friends first. That's what you bloody want, isn't it? To be *friends*." He lingers on the last word, and I can't quite tell if he's trying to embrace it or if he's hoping to obliterate it from the English language.

"Did you talk to the police?"

"Yes. Nothing ever came of it. There were no actual threats. No history of violence. Nothing really to go on, according to them." There's a trace of bitterness in my voice. Nothing but my terror. Which apparently didn't rate at all.

"Did you think he'd hurt you?" Ben's brow is furrowed, his eyes intently upon me. I shift uncomfortably under his gaze.

"I don't know. He seemed deranged. I think anyone who's deranged could be dangerous. It was like he had invented a whole narrative around our relationship that bore no resemblance to reality, and he truly believed it. That was scary."

"What happened?"

"It petered out. It took forever. Maybe eighteen months. Contact got further and further apart. I moved. I changed my mobile number. Hand-dropped notes vanished first. I guess I was harder to find. And security at work all had his photo—there was no chance he'd get into the office. Emails took the longest. I didn't want to change my work email at first. But whenever I blocked an email address he'd just open a new one. Eventually I redirected any unknown contacts to go to Chloe automatically, to screen for me. She took it out of my hands."

"That was good of her." Ben ponders this for a moment. "It can't have been easy. She must have worried."

"She was fine with it. She liked having input." *Control, more likely*, I think to myself, and then feel ungrateful. But I'm sick of this subject already. I don't want to give that fucker one more pathetic, shrivelled-up, stale crumb of my attention.

"And now?"

"I got another letter. It was hand-delivered. To work."

Ben shoots backwards in his chair.

"Christ! Ada. You need to get security back on it. Jesus." He's running his hand through his mop of hair, all traces of flirtation long gone. There's something sexy about his agitation, his focus.

His protectiveness? I wonder to myself. *His love, even?*

"It didn't say anything concerning. Some bullshit about how happy he is. And I should get in touch now before he forgets about me for good if I want to stay connected to him." I laugh, a mirthless bark. "See? Nuts. The guy is fucking nuts."

We're both silent for a moment. Then I say, "Look, I don't want to talk about this anymore. I should never have been with him. It was—" I stop myself abruptly, remembering exactly what it was.

Ben watches me carefully, waiting.

"I need to get back to work. I have articles to finish proofing before tomorrow."

"Like hell you are going back there tonight with no one there. Absolutely not."

I glance at him sharply.

"I can look after myself, actually," I snap. "I'm not going to rearrange my whole life for one idiot. I'll be fine." Then, relenting a little, "I'll lock the doors. And I'll call building security to escort me to the tram stop. And I'll fish out that damn photo. Happy?"

"Not even a little bit," Ben mutters. "What's to say he's not on the tram?"

But I'm already standing up, slapping a ten-dollar note on the table. Ben waves it away in irritation.

"What about dinner? You can't work on a glass of wine."

4

BEN

DESPITE HER PROTESTS, I grab some takeaway and follow Ada back to her office, knocking on her door only minutes behind her.

She's already engrossed in whatever is on her computer screen, a pen in her hand and a thick notebook beside her.

I think about the work waiting for me at my office, but brush it aside. Nothing that can't wait until tomorrow.

Ada works harder than anyone I know. She's cold and prickly as a boss—she has a terrible reputation. Junior staff scatter when she so much as raises an eyebrow at them. Never has disdain been so successfully conveyed with such a minute gesture.

But she's also brilliant and dedicated and a force of nature. She can work ninety hours a week without even noticing. She can guide a staff of over eighty people to produce a magazine in which there is not one corner cut. She loves getting everything perfect. So it irks her to no end that I run my magazine in the completely opposite fashion. My staff are relaxed and no doubt working at significantly less than capacity. The odd typo sneaks through into print. Sometimes a photo gets mixed into the wrong story. But there's laughter and friendship and cavorting in my office, which is just how I like it. I don't mind a few cut corners if everyone is having a good time.

"Are you going to bring that food over here?" she asks, not looking away from her screen.

Behind her, the sun is bouncing off the other skyscrapers in central Melbourne. From her corner office I can see the bay, white sails dotted across it. A giant cruiser is docked at Station Pier. Pink clouds streak across the sky, reflected in the buildings around us.

Wordlessly I pull the noodles from the bag I'm carrying and hand her some chopsticks. She's pulled her hair into a rough bun and kicked off her heels, and is concentrating on the double page spread in front of her. Her head is slightly lowered, the curve of her neck tantalisingly close to me, her full red lips pouty with deliberation. Occasionally she chews on her bottom lip absentmindedly.

Her breasts swell in her shirt magnificently, her plunging neckline revealing an inch of pale blue lace bra from the angle I'm standing at behind her. Her skirt has ridden up her thighs and hugs her hips suggestively.

Without even thinking, I reach out and run a finger along the back of her neck. Her skin is so soft. The short downy hair there is glinting golden in the light. Her bun looks like it's about to fall out, letting her glorious red hair fall down her back. I have the urge to shake it free, grab a fistful of it. Pull her head back and press my lips to hers.

She goes very still, her eyes not moving from the screen.

"What are you doing?" she says, her voice controlled, not an ounce of feeling in it. But I know there's feeling underneath.

"Trying to win you back," I murmur, sweeping my fingertips across her shoulders and down her arms, dropping a soft kiss in the curve of her neck. I ache with how badly I want to touch more of her.

I can see goosebumps spring up across her arms, hear her

breathing quicken. But she says, in that damn flat voice, "Please, Ben. Don't."

My chest squeezes painfully as my hand drops away from her skin.

I drop a kiss on the top of her head and walk away.

5

BEN – 14 YEARS OLD

November 1994

It rained on the day that they were married.

I remember it mainly for the cake.

Everything else felt a bit surreal. I'm sure I must have met Janey earlier, but I can't actually remember it. Saw her that day as a stranger. Some woman looking up at my father, all big smiles and loud laughter.

I don't remember feeling sad or angry or even confused. What I remember is feeling like we were in a movie. And someone would eventually come and call "Cut!" and we'd all go back to our real lives. The real life with my real mother and our rambling, warm house further out of town.

I barely noticed my new siblings. I kicked the toe of one new leather boot—bought specifically for the occasion—against the table leg underneath the long white tablecloth, satisfied by the way the whole table shuddered, the wine bottles clinked.

I didn't know anyone. It was a small gathering, and I learnt later that most of the adults I did know felt that the wedding was too soon. They couldn't celebrate Dad's new love while they were

still grieving for his old one. And me, I still didn't really believe
that Mum was gone.

So I stared at the table and kicked that table leg through the
ceremony, and probably would have kicked it through the
speeches, through the meal, through the entire day had Ada not
slipped into the chair next to me, her hand gentle on my arm. Her
presence soothing and solid and somehow offering camaraderie
on a day when I felt otherwise alone.

6

ADA

"Are we ever going to talk about the giant elephant in the room?"

"No," Chloe says, firmer than I expected. "Let's stick to Kingston and these letters."

"Letter. One letter," I reply in frustration. "And it's all we've spoken about for a week. Can't we talk about something more interesting?"

"No. Not until you've come up with a plan I can get on board with."

"Like calling the police? That's a waste of time. It's not a threatening letter. It's a friendship request! They're not going to do anything. We don't even know that it's from Kingston."

"Why wouldn't it be from him? Who else has ever sent you creepy letters?"

Chloe looks agitated.

Partly because she's worried about me, I know. But partly also because she thinks she knows best, about this, about all things. She's frustrated that I'm not following her Very Sensible Suggestions. Otherwise known as Orders.

"Chloe, can we drop it? We've had this conversation a hundred times. It didn't get us anywhere last time. Let's just skip it this time, okay?"

I mean it to sound encouraging and persuasive, but it comes out wrong, and her head snaps up at me in fury.

"It's not just about you, you know. We were mentioned in those letters. It's unbelievably selfish of you to not take us into account. Our *safety*."

Her words feel like a slap across the face. I snap back, the accusation shattering.

You exposed us to this.

Your poor choices.

Not that it's something new. Something I haven't said to myself a million times. But hearing Chloe say it out loud is shocking somehow. Like I thought I had buried that shame long ago and its re-emergence is devastating.

Because she's right: Kingston's letters post-breakup made no sense, but they did try to assign blame everywhere but on his own shoulders, nevertheless. Chloe was implicated (*"She never liked me. What did she say to you? You always trot along after her like the good little sister. I bet she told you to break it off with me."*). Bill was implicated (*"Your stepdad was always short with me. Did he talk you out of it? I bet he was threatened by my success."*). Even our mother was rebuked through them (*"...if your mother had raised a stronger daughter who could make her own decisions..."*).

Then there were the not-quite threats. Vague and unsettling, because they were so unclear. At least with an outright threat I would have known what I was working with. And maybe could have gotten the police on board.

"You'll all come to a bad end."

"Bad things are coming for people like you."

Did he mean, by virtue of our imagined colluding—excluding him, deeming him unworthy—that we'd all fall prey to karma?

Or did he mean that he was plotting, at that very moment, exactly what kind of "bad end" he would coordinate for us all?

I never responded, so I never got any more clarity. It just hung over us all, clammy and dank. And it's one thing to put myself in harm's way, but quite another to bring it on my family.

"That was years ago. This one didn't mention any of you. You're overreacting."

I hate that my mistake brought this on them. It makes me defensive and snappy and throws me to the other end of the argument. Particularly with Chloe. For some reason, every strong statement she ever makes sees me hurl myself behind the opposite conviction. I know I'm doing it. Even I don't believe what I am saying. But somehow, 37 years of sistering rears its ugly head in times of stress. I react the way I always have.

I wonder if she does, too.

"Is that supposed to make me feel better? We should just wait and see what he says or does next?"

I feel suddenly exhausted again. I feel like I've had conversations in a similar vein with Chloe all my life. When there's nothing to disagree on, she's the most supportive, funny, and reliable sister in the world.

When we don't see eye to eye, she tries to bully me into doing what she wants.

"We see it differently," I say, trying to summon a more adult response, but resigned to the dismissal this line will be met with. We might see it differently, but where I can understand Chloe's point of view—stand in her shoes, roll her perspective around in my head to get a feel for it—she rarely troubles herself with trying to understand mine.

Thankfully, we're interrupted by the arrival of Mum and Bill. But my relief is short-lived; Chloe is straight back into it with them.

"Will you two please talk some sense into my little sister?" she says. The diminutive reference isn't lost on me. She's trying to imply that as the eldest, *of course* she knows better. It's infuriating.

Bill smiles at me helplessly. Mum raises her eyebrows in question.

"I got a letter that *might* be from Kingston," I say in irritation. It's going to come out soon enough anyway.

Mum's look of alarm surprises me. But I just don't have the energy. I let their conversation drift over my head as I sip my wine and think about all the things I could be doing back at the office. These never-ending family get-togethers are maddening. No one I know "catches up" as often as my family.

Last time I tried to suggest that to my mother, and wriggle out of attendance, she had said, "But we're *family*. It's *fun*. I *want* to see you."

"What about what I want?" I had grumbled back.

"You want to check things off your to-do list," she had laughed. "We're trying to save you from achieving it all too soon and having nothing left to live for." She was being good-natured, but it was a little too close to home. Fun for me *was* achieving things on my to-do list.

"Ada? What do you think?" Bill's gentle voice brings me back to the present.

I haven't been listening, but I can take a pretty good stab at what's he's asking.

"Look. I'm not happy that he was at the office. But the police aren't going to do anything. I think we should be alert, not alarmed." I cackle to myself at the government terrorism motto. No one else laughs, though, and I sigh, wondering where Ben is. Though I suppose he would be contributing to the worry, not diffusing it in his usual manner.

"I just want to forget about him, okay? My work email has changed and it isn't publicly listed. It's not one of those ones that is easy to guess. I'll have my PA check my snail mail and send any more letters to you, Chloe. And you guys can decide what to do with them. Okay?"

Mum and Chloe glance at each other, but I pointedly turn back to the menu. "Let's order," I say. "I have to go back to the office to finish a few things up tonight." More glances are exchanged, but I don't care. Working makes me happy. It happens to make me a lot of money, too. So they can glance at each other as much as they like. This dinner is the "work" for me.

The office is the fun bit.

7

ADA – 15 YEARS OLD

JANUARY 1995

Chloe is rifling through my wardrobe, pulling out my recently and rarely acquired new tops and holding them against her, one by one, trying some on and then discarding them in a pile on the floor beside her.

My heart is thumping in my chest, the effort of trying to find the right words and get them out of my mouth feeling like a war going on inside me.

Chloe is so kind to me. She lets me hang out with her older, cooler friends. She checks in on me to make sure I'm okay when Dad misses another of my birthdays or calls her and doesn't ask to speak to me.

She tries to lure me out on weekends, genuinely worried that I spend too much time with my books and not enough time having fun, being a teenager. She'll plan fun excursions and promise we'll only go for an hour or two, that I won't miss too much study. And she's careful to stick to her word, keeping a watchful eye on my rising agitation, which increases in direct correlation to the time spent away. She knows when it's time to deliver me safely back to my desk.

But.

She also takes my things without asking, spills red wine on my new tops, ruins my cassette tapes in her car's old and unreliable tape player, returning them in a tangled, crinkled, useless mess. And she feigns oblivion when I try to ask her to be more careful.

In some strange way, I feel like she's asking if she's important enough. If I'll love her enough to share with her. It's a feeling I can't shake. And so my heart thumps, and I think this time I'll say something, get angry, be firmer. And then I don't. Because I recognise that need. I'm constantly asking it of my mother. Never getting back the reassuring answer that I want. That I matter. That I'm worth it.

So Chloe—she can borrow my clothes. Stretch them. Feign ignorance. Get the answer that she needs.

Later, with a heavy heart, I slowly hang my crumpled new clothes back on their hangers. And wonder if I'm imagining it all.

8

BEN

November 16, 2017

"You won her back yet?" Lucas is peering at me over a whiskey, his grin not in the slightest bit comforting or helpful. He thinks this is a giant joke.

To be fair, he thinks Ada is my perfect match, and this is just a small blip in our relationship. A hurdle that Ada needs to overcome—and that overcoming it is inevitable. He has spent so much time with us. He can't believe we won't sort this out.

"I'm working on it," I reply, not sharing his conviction.

"For the guy who told me to get on it and sort it out regarding *my* love life, you seem to be moving remarkably slowly on your own," he drawls.

"How is Clara?" I'm swirling my glass, watching the thick amber liquid go round and round, the ice clinking, my thoughts elsewhere.

"She's great. But we're not talking about her."

I sigh deeply. I seem to be doing that a lot these days. "Look, she's got a point. Her mother would have a fit if she knew about Ada and me. And my dad would have a fit in response. Honestly, I don't think he'd care if Janey didn't. But he takes his lead from her. And she cares *a lot* about what people think. You've met the woman. She's so damn into appearances."

Lucas frowns. "I just don't get why it's a big deal. You're not related. You didn't even meet 'til you were what, fourteen? Fifteen? You hardly grew up together. And doesn't this kind of thing happen all the time?"

"I have no idea. But it freaks Ada right the fuck out. She reckons Janey would consider it incest. And though frankly I don't really care what Janey thinks, Ada's really hung up on it. She's on a perpetual quest to win her mum's approval. God knows why. What Janey approves of is always shifting with her latest fad. For a while her approval was completely tied up in healthy living and meditating. Which lasted all of five weeks. It's all she talked about, and she banged on and on about getting Ada started on some liver-cleansing bollocks and morning meditation. She actually does not give the slightest shit about what matters to Ada."

I suddenly realise I'm getting louder and crosser with each word, as the woman at the next table glances at me disapprovingly. I lower my voice.

"But Ada keeps trying anyway. And not shaming the family is an umbrella goal. You know what Ada's like. Everything has to be ticked and crossed and frog-marched to its proper place. And concreted in for good measure."

"That hasn't stopped her being with you for twenty years," Lucas counters. "So she's obviously okay with it. I really wouldn't have taken Ada for someone who cares so much about what other people think."

"Not other people," I say wearily. "Just her mother."

It's hard to explain to Lucas. It's like Ada and I have the history of siblings; we can see each other's behaviour through a lens that feels clearer than how the other person views it themselves. Most of the time that means I'm the person Ada turns to for support. But maybe I don't really get it. Maybe believing that I get it is just arrogance on my part.

"She's been tunnel-visioned for as long as I've known her," I say, trying to explain. "She was always trying to be the best at everything. And I don't think she was competitive. I don't think she cared about winning for herself. I think the only time she ever got Janey's attention was when she won something. And it lasted all of five seconds. Then Janey would be on to the next shiny thing. And instead of that making her give up, it just made her drive stronger. She still does it. Whenever I try to talk to her about it, she gets really pissed. But I think she's still hoping if she does everything perfectly, Janey will actually really pay attention to her or something. I dunno...their relationship...it's a bit fucked up."

Lucas is staring pensively at his whiskey, and I start guiltily. "Shit, sorry dude. I wasn't thinking."

We're silent for a few moments, then I add, "Have you spoken to her at all?"

Lucas shakes his head. "You don't need to be sorry. It's weird, though, the different levels of parent shitness. And kind of scary, if you think about having kids. Like, fuck. Does anyone get it right? Janey seems fun and loving and kind from the outside. She seems a million times nicer than my mum. And Ada still sounds fucked up about her."

"Said like the fiancé of a therapist," I laugh. "You know, I think it got worse after Kingston. I'm not just saying that 'cause I want to kill the fucker, either." I grin at Lucas, then frown again. "But she's much more obsessive now about doing everything herself. She used to delegate stuff with the magazine and skive off with me, at least some of the time. She hasn't really done that since their fling. Got agitated if I even suggested it. And she was obsessed about one typo in the magazine a few months ago. Like, anyone would have thought she printed something libellous or accidentally put a fairy tale in instead of some steamy adult content. She was really beside herself. Like, devastated out of all proportion."

I ponder this for a little while. *Is Ada more uptight than she used to be?*

"Sounds exhausting. Hasn't she noticed that everyone makes mistakes?" Lucas interrupts my thoughts. "Jeez, if I fell in a hole every time I made a mistake I'd be halfway to China by now. Sometimes mistakes deserve forgiveness, not self-immolation. How else are you supposed to learn?"

"Yeah." Suddenly I'm sick of this subject. She's not even my woman anymore. Now that I think about it, she's been both getting more obsessive *and* pushing me away since Kingston. So maybe she's right. Maybe it is time to move on. To someone less complicated.

But even as I think it, my stomach clenches in protest.

No one else comes even close to Ada. She might be complicated. But she's everything to me.

I just don't know how to make her see how little the step-thing matters.

9

ADA

November 17, 2017

Chloe raps on my door a little louder than is required.

Her shoulders are set in a stiff line, her chin out.

I sigh, leaning back in my chair.

"Is this a closed-door kind of conversation?" I ask, without preamble. I don't really want the whole office hearing about Kingston.

She pauses in her advance and backtracks to shut the door.

"I've had a talk with Mum, and we've decided we need to talk to the police again," she announces, dumping her handbag on my desk atop my proofs. It's almost like a challenge.

Sometimes it's easier to humour Chloe than to fight her.

"Fine," I say. "You do it."

She looks surprised.

"What? Braced for battle, were we?"

She grins and rolls her eyes. Now that she has my agreement, she's all smiles again.

"Well, I thought you might take some convincing."

"I don't have the time or the energy. But you do what you

like," I tell her, plucking her bag off my desk and plonking it to the floor next to her feet.

She drops into the chair behind me, tucking her legs underneath her, flopping her head back so she's staring at the ceiling.

"Good. With some of the threats in the earlier letters, and the fact that this was hand-delivered, I'm sure we can get some kind of action."

She's completely wrong. The police aren't going to do a damn thing. But it's easier to let her learn that for herself.

BACK AT HOME, I lean my forehead against the fridge.

It's 9:25 p.m. and there's nothing interesting in my house to eat. I wish I'd grabbed some takeaway on the way home.

Instead, I pull a single-serve frozen dhal out of the freezer from a pile of many. Pre-mixed with rice, it's the perfect size. Easy. Healthy. Not too filling. I don't like feeling full, and thus sleepy or sluggish, just in case something comes up and I need to do some work.

I stare at the little frozen package in dissatisfaction, before putting it in the microwave. There's easily two dozen more of them in the freezer. I like to kid myself that they're for nights like this, when I get home late, when I can't be bothered cooking. But basically I eat them every night.

I read *The Rosie Project* recently. I rarely read these days, unless it's related to an article we're running. It was a rare treat. A silver lining to the gap in my life left by Ben.

Usually, he'd come round on a Friday night. Too tired for games, we'd both collapse on the couch. Cuddle like a real couple. Eat takeaway and drink nice wine. Enjoy the silence.

I sigh and open the fridge. Pull out a half-empty bottle of white. Pour a large glass. Feel a little bit wistful.

I laughed out loud throughout that book. More than I had laughed in months. Years, maybe. But I was left with the image of what's-his-name and his meals by day of the week.

I was even more rigid. I made enough for a bloody month and ate it religiously. One bloody single-serve at a time.

Was this funny? Pragmatic?

Or a little bit weird?

I'm distracted by my phone pinging.

It's our night.

Ben.

My heart hurts a little bit thinking about him. But I ignore the message and sit down with my dhal and wine. And a different kind of silence.

10

ADA – 17 YEARS OLD

November 1997

I'm crying when Ben comes in.

"Don't you knock anymore?" I snap, pretending I'm cross, not upset. Hoping he won't notice. "I said no already!"

Honestly. Our final mathematics exam this afternoon and he wants to go study in the park. I hunch over my textbook, twirling my pen pointedly.

He's tilting his head, trying to see my face, but I let my hair fall across the pages in front of me, shielding my puffy eyes from his scrutiny.

"You've been studying for hours," he says softly. "Look at your graph."

Embarrassed, I shove the graph into a drawer. Its neatly ruled lines, tracking my daily study hours—climbing steadily over the past three months—suddenly seems obsessive, even to me.

"I really admire your dedication," he goes on, gently rubbing my shoulders. "But you've got to eat too. I was just seeing if I could make you a sandwich? Our folks have headed off for the weekend."

Oh. He's not hassling me to go to the park.

A sob escapes me, despite my best efforts, and I shake my head, trying to shake my stupid feelings away. Ben is the last person I want to see me blubbering. I like how he sees me: witty and playful and strong.

"Hey, hey," he says, coming round to my side, brushing my hair away from my face. "What's wrong, Adds?"

"I'm just really tired," I tell him. "I just want this exam to be over. But a sandwich would be great. Thanks."

He doesn't leave though. Just watches me quietly.

"Wanna talk about it?" he asks eventually.

I can't help myself. My face crumples. Unattractively, I imagine. But I can't hold it in any longer. Especially given he has known me all of two and a half years, and sees me more clearly than my own mother.

"It will sound so stupid. Childish," I start, my voice cracking and squeaking. Just trying to form the sentences undoes me.

"Shh, shh," Ben soothes, pulling me to him, stroking my hair. I can feel his warm breath on my neck, his broad chest rising and falling against me. He feels so solid, so dependable.

Unlike my mother.

How could she just leave like that? She didn't even say, "Good luck." It's only the subject I struggle with the most. Bloody maths.

But somehow, under Ben's fingers, it doesn't seem so bad anymore.

Eventually I pull backwards, smile at him, wipe my wet eyes with my sleeve.

"Sorry," I mutter. "I just heard the car leave. That stupid toot she always does, leaving the driveway. As though there isn't twenty bloody yards of clear vision on either side."

Ben waits, not speaking but watching me. He somehow manages to create such a nice, safe space wherever he goes.

"It just shows how little I matter, you know?" I shrug. "She was always like this. She just never holds me in mind. Like, she'll be gone for three nights. You'd think she could manage,

"Goodbye, good luck with your maths final." She'll bloody expect me to top the class."

I stare down at my desk, suddenly tired. Suddenly sick of her mattering so much. Sick of trying and trying and trying to please her, and it not making the slightest, smallest bit of difference.

"Come on," I say, looking up at Ben. "Let's get that sandwich."

Anything to move on to something else.

11

ADA

November 20, 2017

A few days later Mum pops into my office unannounced, her modus operandi.

"I have a team meeting in ten," I tell her, not bothering with greetings. I've told her a million times to call before visiting.

"I just had lunch with Chloe." She gestures out the window, to the city in general, like that will illuminate me on something. I wait.

"She spoke to the police. They weren't very helpful. We'll have to come up with another plan."

"Can it wait? I need to finalise a couple of things for the meeting."

"Just take your laptop, darling. You're always on top of everything. I'm sure you'll be fine."

"I'm on top of everything because I plan and prepare," I say through gritted teeth. "I don't like to go into meetings late or unprepared."

"Well, I'll make it quick then," she says, but the woman is incapable of conveying anything quickly. She perches on the edge of my desk, picks up a frame, and frowns.

"This is an odd thing to have on your desk, darling," she says, tapping the glass accusingly. "Can't you put a nice family picture in here or something?"

"You were going to be quick, I think?" I prompt her, thinking that a family picture is the last thing I'd want on my desk. Except of Ben, perhaps. But that would be harder to explain than the reprint in there that came with the frame, a gift from an intern upon her departure. I've enjoyed annoying Jason with it for months. "I haven't found the right picture yet," I tell him, deadpan. He finally caught on, started to laugh.

"Oh, yes." Still she stares at the frame, in no hurry at all to tell me what she wants and let me get to my meeting on time. I grind my teeth together to stop myself from saying something unkind. Which has never helped in the past. Any complaints I've ever raised about her self-absorbed behaviour have been *my* problems, *my* issues that I need to deal with. And she'll be waiting with love and fucking forgiveness when I've worked them out.

It's infuriating trying to have a relationship with someone who has no insight whatsoever and no inclination to get any.

Finally she puts the frame down and looks up. "It's about Bill's birthday. You do know it's his seventieth next month? I'm trying to plan a surprise for him. I can't quite decide what yet. I wanted to run some ideas past you. And I know you and Ben are close; maybe you can talk to him about it and help me work out something great. A present? A holiday? You two are right on the pulse of all the trendy things, aren't you?" She gestures grandly again, encompassing not just all of my magazine paraphernalia, but all of Melbourne in a sweeping motion.

I wish she would be more specific.

She stands up and starts wandering unhurriedly around the room, looking at the sparse artwork on the walls, the shelves crammed full of books and magazines. She hasn't worked for as long as I can remember. Keeps a rich husband and has no idea what is involved in running a business. Why I can't jump to accommodate her whims for unreasonable things at late notice.

"Gosh, you have so many magazines in here. You could start a secondhand store. Maybe I could borrow some? Always nice to have some coffee-table reading on cold days."

"Mum. Please. I am leaving this office in three minutes." I can no longer keep the impatience out of my voice.

"Well. No need to get snappy." She frowns at me. "I've been spending my time trying to sort out this mess with Kingston, something you seem hell-bent on ignoring. A little reciprocation would be nice."

"Leaving, Mum," I tell her, striving to keep my voice light and calm but seething with rage inside. I start gathering up papers and notes for the meeting, then pointedly hold the door open for her. No way am I leaving her in this office without me.

She wanders breezily toward the door, refusing to be hurried. As though an afterthought, she pauses. "Perhaps you could do an article about him in the magazine? Something celebrating his life? Now *that* would be special. Not many people would get that for their seventieth!"

I stare at her. Even after fifteen years, she still has no idea what running my magazine entails or what my readers are interested in. Bill is lovely—why on earth he is with my mother still escapes me—but without the abs of a rock god, or some steamy scandal to report on, he's about as interesting to my demographic as a celibate toad.

"Is he a billionaire banker with a foot fetish and some tips to share with young women who want to offer their feet up for adulation, in exchange for a pile of money? Or perhaps there's a scandal with a teenage celebrity we can get the scoop on?" I tilt my head to the side, seeing the anger flashing in her eyes. I don't think I've ever made fun of her before.

Something about it feels remarkably, unsettlingly good.

12

BEN

WHEN I WANDER into my office on Monday morning, there's an intern sobbing in my recliner.

I stop abruptly just inside the door, and turn and raise a questioning eyebrow back at Rich, my PA, who shrugs apologetically. I leave the door open, indicating it slightly with my head. Hopeful interns have thrown themselves at me in the past. With a remarkable ability to shed their clothes between being seated talking to me about a problem and being in front of me with a proposition.

"Stace, what's up?" Her long, blonde hair is covering her face, her short dress not covering much of her legs. She peeks up at me through long, black lashes.

"Julia cancelled my interview. I'm so disappointed. I've been researching for days. I felt like this article could have been my break, have people take me seriously as a writer," she wails, a little too overdone, all things considered.

Sometimes I wonder if Ada's approach is actually not so bad, after all. I really don't have time to reassure a nineteen-year-old intern whilst simultaneously ensuring she doesn't try to transition reassurance into comforting into full-frontal nudity.

I sit down at my desk, leaning toward her with warmth and concern, but clearly conveying that this won't be a touching kind of reassurance; there's a good few feet between us. Then I go through the usual—it's early days; this happens all the time; it's important to learn how to bounce back and move on to the next thing; consider it all part of her learning experience here. The ex-Prime Minister has to manage her brand carefully. Perhaps her people felt our magazine wasn't really a good fit (which is actually the case, but I don't say that). The important thing is how she deals with the disappointment. Yada yada yada.

When I finally usher her out, urging her to speak to her supervisor about her work plan for the next few days, Rich raises an eyebrow at me. "You've got more patience than me," he mutters when she's out of earshot.

"Don't want to crush their spirits." I grin at him. "But we really need to find a way to make my office a bit more of a closed-door arrangement."

"How about you stop being so bloody charming?" he replies, reproachful.

"You mean, 'interested in my staff's work and approachable about problems,'" I laugh, thrumming my knuckles on his desk. "Probably I'm in the wrong job. Talking to people is the part I like. Running this damn thing..." I trail off. I really do miss getting out, interviewing people, the banter with colleagues. It's kind of lonely in my huge, glass-walled office. Hence the chatting to staff out on the floor. And hence their subsequent feeling that I'm the person they can and should talk to about every bloody damn thing that crops up.

On the flipside, holding the top job has given me years of excuses to see Ada. And oh, seeing Ada as a rival? I wouldn't have traded those visits to her office for the world.

THE FIRST TIME we had sex was on her eighteenth birthday.

Even then, she knew what she wanted.

Later—much later—she confessed she had planned the whole evening out. She had set out to seduce me. And like everything else in her life, the evening ran completely to her plan.

She had thought of everything.

I was hardly an unwilling participant though. Two horny teenagers thrust into close proximity like that? I had never had such opportunities to get close to a girl who I actually liked. An *unrelated* girl, I had kept telling myself, as I lounged on her bed discussing homework or bitching about the ruthless maths teacher, her long, smooth legs thrown carelessly over my lap, or her head nestled under my arm, chatting and musing for hours on end. Pretending to giggle over her literary crushes. (As far as I know, she never had a crush on any actual boys in high school. But I was wildly jealous of even the fictional ones.) Watching her dry her hair and apply makeup in the shared bathroom on the rare occasion she left the house. As she chatted about what she and her girlfriends were doing that evening.

I'd been in love with her pretty much since that first year living together. She was my complete opposite. Studious and quiet to my laid-back and gregarious. She hid in the background at family events and I entertained the crowd. She cared so much about her school results and I thought, "she'll be right," about pretty much everything. Getting good grades, getting into university—I figured it would all work out in the end. I didn't consider for a moment working toward something with the fervour that Ada did.

But when it was just the two of us, alone in her bedroom, she was the funniest girl I had ever met.

I took it to mean she wasn't afraid of me, like she seemed afraid of everyone else. Which seems odd, now, with her entire staff terrified of her. But she's not mean. She just has exacting standards and can't bear stupidity, especially if it affects her end product.

Back then, though, her dry humour and her quick wit matched my own. I felt like they belonged to me, in a way. No one else ever saw them. They were like a precious gift that she brought out just for me.

And, of course, she was utterly gorgeous. That red hair. Those smooth legs. She was already curvy, with lush, pouty lips and delicious tits.

That helped my crush somewhat too.

So yeah. I'd been in love with her for a good three years by the time she turned eighteen.

But it was Ada who had the balls to act on it.

Quiet, studious Ada.

She ruined me for every other girl who might have come after.

No wonder I can't let her go.

She was so confident.

She was everything.

I pick up a photo of us, before that first time.

We look innocent and over-excited: wide smiles, arms flung around each other's necks, eyes squinting at the camera. Young and carefree.

Ada's face gives away nothing. No hint of the carefully planned events that must have been at the forefront of her mind. And no hint of concern about her mother's reaction if she ever found out what Ada had planned for the evening.

Throwing it all away now because she's worried about her mother disowning her doesn't even add up. If she was so worried about that, why did she even start this thing between us? Surely it would have been worse when we were eighteen than now, when we're independent adults who aren't even that close to our parents?

Surely we can work it out?

13

BEN – 18 YEARS OLD

MAY 1998

Ada came down the stairs, tossing her red mane over her shoulder—all those shiny, silken, glowing threads dancing in the light.

I pretended to focus on the Stubbs painting at the foot of the stairs, trying not to ogle her. I thought she was beautiful anyway, but I'd never seen her dressed like this. The heels, the dress, the shiny lips. Legs that went on forever.

We were going to a club to celebrate her birthday—just a few days after mine.

I jokingly asserted that with all my worldly wisdom—eighteen a whole four days ahead of her—that I could "show her the scene." She had laughed, her head falling back, something striking me as strange about how carefree she seemed, despite her disappointment that none of her friends could make it (later, of course, she confessed that she'd invited not a single one of them).

She was wearing this tiny silver dress that was basically backless. With her hair swept over one shoulder, I stared at her flawless back as she walked to the taxi, dumbstruck by the sight of her. The firm lines of her butt under the caress of the dress. The way it rode deliciously, provocatively up so I could see a flash of her skimpy underwear when she leaned down to greet the taxi driver.

Not knowing she'd even planned that part, too, adjusting her wardrobe mirrors and perfecting the angle of the lean over so it was just right. Just enough to make me think of sex. In case I'd never thought of her that way before.

If only she knew.

I hurried to the front seat, not sure I could keep my hands off her in the back.

I imagined grabbing her hair, yanking her head back to expose her creamy neck. The way I wanted to kiss it. The way I wanted to pull her ass against my cock. I spent the whole taxi ride with my hands across my lap, terrified, excited. Hoping the driver wouldn't notice my raging hard-on.

Inside the club the music was thrumming loudly, strobe lights over the dance floor messing with my concentration. Completely oblivious to her plans, I tried to focus on staying sober and brotherly. I might have jerked off a thousand times to the image of her glorious tits bouncing over our bathroom sink as I rammed my cock into her from behind, but I would never, in a million years, have made the first move.

Then there was Ada. Thoughtful, good girl Ada.

Sensible, overachieving Ada, planning this evening so impeccably.

Setting us up for two decades of the most mind-blowing sex that I couldn't have imagined in my wildest, wildest dreams.

She took my hand once we were inside, pulling me up to the bar, sliding her perfect, barely covered arse onto a barstool, one knee casually angled between my legs, our knees touching. She looked so demure, but her legs were parted just enough for me to see her thighs virtually all the way up to her underwear. And once my eyes started travelling that way, I had no hope in hell of stopping my mind following. *Those thighs. What underwear is she wearing? Does she shave? What does she look like down there?* It was all I could do not to fall to my knees between her legs to find out then and there.

And still I had no idea she was directing the scene like a professional. I was a complete hack, but under her magical direction, I sang my lines like a star.

Later, after many drinks, Ada led me to the dance floor.

I tried to keep my distance, my eyes lingering on her, helplessly drawn to her hips, her lips, her shimmering hair—then darting away in a panic.

Girls seemed to like me. And I had fooled around a bit, sure. Had my hands in all sorts of interesting places. But not with Ada. And none of those girls...well, they were no Ada. They didn't make my heart gallop and my breathing ragged.

They didn't make my thinking foggy and my stomach somersault.

I had never thought that being with her was possible.

But that night, I couldn't think of anything else.

And Ada...Ada attracted attention. Under the disco lights, she was lit up like a shooting star, her hair and her dress and her shoes sparkling to such perfection that you could be forgiven for thinking the club was paying her to give them some extra pull. And when other guys started circling closer and closer, openly eyeing her arse and her bouncing breasts, jostling each other out of the way like sharks circling their next victim, Ada pulled me in close to her.

"Pretend you're with me," she had whispered in my ear, her breath hot against my skin, the smell of her perfume and shampoo and just *her*—intoxicating. It was the smell of friendship and closeness and easy banter, but also the smell of sex and desire and intrigue and woman. I had tried to pull back, an automatic reaction from somewhere deep inside me that knew I couldn't survive such proximity without my innermost desires spilling out all over the dance floor, plain for everyone, including Ada, to see. But she held me determinedly, pulling me hard against her, our bodies touching from our interlocking thighs all the way up to her breasts, which pushed insistently into my chest.

Who the fuck was this girl?

Not the do-gooder Ada I knew and loved, silently, from afar.

This Ada was intentional and assertive.

This Ada was smoking hot—and I was getting lost in her.

Second by second, my determination to be a good friend to her was melting away.

I closed my eyes. Ada's body was pressed all over me. The booze and the heat and my desire were everywhere.

I held her tightly, stroking her waist with my thumb. Trying to pretend it was all an act, to ward off the circling men, but my cock was springing to life, bulging unmistakably against her. For a moment I was terrified. But if anything, she held me even tighter. Pressed herself into my cock, her arms around my torso, my neck. Her hips moving to the music, grinding against me. Her hands never stopped moving. She looked up at me, smiling, our eyes locking.

Then with deliberate slowness, she pressed her lips to mine.

14

ADA

November 22, 2017

I know what you get up to with your brother.

That's all it says.

Typed to look as though it's on a typewriter. Addressed to me, but delivered to Chloe's address.

She's hysterical, obviously—*"He knows where I live, Ada! He knows where I LIVE!!"* She sent me a photo, but took the offending item straight to the police station, promising to demand some action.

"You can't tell Mum what it says," I had told her, my heart erratic in my chest, my breath painfully short, a headache creeping around my temple, sly and relentless. My office had suddenly felt small and dense.

She'd screamed at me. Incoherently, mostly. Ending with, "You only ever fucking think about yourself!" Hanging up.

It was hard to explain to her. Everything suddenly felt so uncertain, so shaky. Like the very ground beneath my feet was in fact not ground at all, but a tightrope, or tiny blocks of ice in a vast, vast sea.

I don't want Mum to know about Ben and me, no. That's part of the problem. A big part.

But there's something else.

I don't think that these latest letters are from Kingston.

For one thing, they're completely different. Short and sharp and printed, compared to the pages and pages of the handwritten nonsense he wrote last time.

And for another thing...I'm pretty sure he's dead.

15

ADA – 33 YEARS OLD

I met Kingston under a tree.

"Kingston," he'd said, offering me his hand. His dark eyebrows quirked upwards, matching his lips. Perfect, full, kissable lips. Day-old stubble graced his angular jaw.

I had looked around awkwardly.

"Uh, yes?" I'd replied, unsure of what he wanted. For a confused moment, I had thought he was asking me for a biscuit. *Kingstons,* I'd thought to myself. *Why does he think I have Kingstons?* Followed closely by: *Who asks a stranger for a biscuit?*

I was sitting against a tree in the botanical gardens, looking down the gently sloping hill, gnawing on the end of my pen, notebook on my lap, brainstorming ideas.

Vague memories of an indistinct man flashing me very near that spot in my early twenties predisposed me to uneasiness. *Weird guy asking for biscuits!!* Some internal danger sign was definitely lighting up at that point.

I should have bloody taken note.

"You're under my tree," he'd said, by way of explanation. "I thought I'd say hi rather than sulk about it." He'd grinned at me and plopped down beside me, charming and boyish. Dark locks flopped across his forehead, reminding me painfully of someone else I knew. Someone who I'd rather not think about.

My thoughts always being hopelessly circular on that particular subject.

I shouldn't be with Ben. It can never go anywhere. I've got to stop it.

"Oh." I had stared at him, his friendliness irking me. I had articles to finalise. I'd never seen the appeal of chatting with random strangers anywhere. Let alone when they were clearly otherwise inclined.

I'd stood up abruptly. "All yours, then," I'd said, brushing grass and twigs off my skirt, striding away from him purposefully. Chiselled jawline or not, the selfishness of interrupting someone who was clearly busy doing something else should not be rewarded, as far as I was concerned.

"Wait, wait," he'd said, scrabbling to his feet, his long legs accentuated by black skinny jeans, his dark eyes catching mine as I glanced back toward him. But I kept walking.

He had fallen in beside me, hands in his back pockets, and we strode silently alongside each other for a while. Finally I had stopped to face him.

"What?"

I was wanting him to fuck off, so I could find another tree. I'd left the office to avoid talking. Even with my door shut, the murmur of my staff through the walls grated on my nerves.

"Date me," he'd replied, his white teeth perfect, flashing beneath his smile.

Looking back, it's easy to make excuses.

He was explosively good-looking.

He wanted me.

It wasn't his stupid tree. He'd seen me there, he said, and had to make me his.

He was so certain. So unequivocal. He was so convinced that he carried enough for the two of us.

But mostly, *mostly*—he wasn't Ben.

16

BEN

November 22, 2017

Chloe: *FIX YOUR SHIT*

The text message is the first time Chloe has ever been confrontational.

She's never even come close before.

I hand Lucas my phone, and he stares at the photo of the letter and Chloe's message beneath it.

"Wow," Lucas says. "And Ada says she's refused to ever talk about it?"

"Yeah. As far as I know. Ignorance is bliss or something, maybe."

"Do you think she'll show that to her mum?"

"Possibly. She's pretty pissed about the whole thing. It was left in her mailbox, so fair enough, she's freaked out. But I don't know that he really has any beef with her. Still. Creepy guy at your mailbox. Yeah...I can see why she's upset."

We're silent for a moment, something bothering me that I can't quite put my finger on.

"It's just—it seems odd, you know? Ada says she hasn't heard from him in a couple of years. Why now? Ada's just broken it off with me. It just doesn't seem to make sense."

"Cause stalkers are always so rational," Lucas says dryly, handing my phone back. "How does Chloe expect you to fix it, anyway? This isn't your shit. Maybe the guy is jealous of you being with Ada, but it's not your fault he's a nutcase. What does she expect you to do?"

"Be all manly and take the guy out?"

"Ha!" Lucas smirks.

"What?!" I say, mock pissed. "You don't think I can protect my woman?"

He laughs, and his laughter lightens my mood.

I'm definitely not the guy that takes anyone out. I soothe crying interns, while carefully avoiding outright rejecting them and leaving them feeling awkward.

I see my people uncomfortable and I fix it.

I like being that guy.

Beating my chest and staking my territory?

No. Not me.

17

BEN – 18 YEARS OLD

MAY 1998

We were actually kissing.

Our tongues danced around each other, gently at first, then deeply, our mouths hungry, probing, locked together as though to separate would be to die, our hands just as ravenous, touching and gripping and grabbing as though time might run out and we hadn't touched everything. My hands found her arse, yanking her into my hard-on, desperate and out of control.

Later, she told me she had these romantic ideas about her first time, her plan to lure me back to her room, how we'd talk and play soft music and kiss slowly and deeply. And how utterly ridiculous the idea was once our lips connected.

"I just wanted your cock inside me already," she said, three, four, five months later. "It was like my life was nothing until that moment. I wanted you so badly and my body wouldn't wait."

STUMBLING AND PANTING, kissing and touching and grabbing at each other the entire way, we somehow found our way out of the club and into the adjoining alley.

"We mustn't," I told her once, even as my thumb slipped inside her panties and stroked the wet fullness of her slit, a groan escaping her lips as I pushed her back further, further, further into a dark little enclave, yanking her knee up to my hips, wrapping her calf around me. Opening her up to me, two fingers stroked the length of her, and I marvelled at how wet she was for me, her panting in my ear driving me wild.

She clawed at my jeans zipper, desperate, fumbling. Her desire was like fireworks. My brain, my body, my life was drenched in perfection. Ada. Wanting me. Her dress up around her waist, my fingers gripping her butt, one strap from her dress yanked down, my hands trying to do everything at once because I wanted to touch every part of her and I only had two hands, one mouth. And every part of her entire body was begging for me to touch it, lick it, claim it.

Freeing a nipple, her bra pulled down, her glorious breast thrust skyward by the material bunched beneath it, I took it roughly into my mouth, sucking hard, my other hand leaving her arse to find the other breast, massaging its heavy fullness, while Ada finally managed to push my pants down. My cock sprung free and she groaned, grasping the shaft and guiding my head toward her slit, pulling her panties to the side, no time to even stop and step out of them, her desperation and hunger matching mine. All thoughts of being friends were long gone. I just wanted to bury my cock so deep inside her and keep it there for the rest of my life.

As I pushed against her, her slick lips parting deliciously, we both groaned. I grabbed her hair and yanked her head back, burying my face in her neck, sucking her skin, licking her, pulling her leg up further still. I remember how it felt as my cock tried to push inside her, crying out with the pleasure of it, the desperation. She was so tight and so wet. I could barely fit. I had to push and thrust, grunting, holding her hips. It felt incredible. And I wasn't even inside her yet.

She grabbed at my ass, pulling me into her, moaning and panting, her lips finding mine again, our mouths working wetly together, tongues pulling and pushing, wild with our need to be connected by as many body parts as possible.

"You're so tight!" I had groaned into her neck, pulling back, marvelling at the wonder of her, the logistics of sex surprising but not as terrifying as I had imagined. I had worried about needing to appear that I knew what I was doing. But with Ada, it didn't matter. It was all perfect. Every single second.

In the end we had to lie down. And finally I was inside her, thrilled by her whimpers and moans, her wet tightness, feeling my cock so deep in her, her stretching as I filled her. Pushing in and out, my butt clenching under her desperate grasp, my enormous need. Our breathing heavy, filling the darkness around us.

The sensation was beyond belief. Anyone could hear us, our pleasure, but my entire world had reduced to this: my cock, sliding in and out of her; her tongue in my mouth, desiring me; her wanting my cock, needing it. Wanting to do everything with her body at once, but not wanting to stop this perfection, ever.

Wanting this moment to go on forever.

Of course, it was over pretty quickly.

Ada was gasping, still writhing against me, and I understood she wanted more. I hesitated. I had managed to give a girl an orgasm with my fingers once before, I think, but I really had no idea what I was doing. My cock slipped out of her, and I was suddenly aware of my bare arse, the gravelly road beneath her, the chances of someone stumbling across us. But Ada wasn't phased.

"Here," she said, taking my fingers, placing them at the top of her slit. "I'll show you what to do."

18

ADA

NOVEMBER 22, 2017

Ben: *I'm coming over.*

The text message interrupts my thoughts. The usual, unhelpful picking apart of what I missed. Going over interactions with Kingston like some clue might be thrown up, some glaring flaw that suddenly explained everything. Because if there was a flaw, a sign, *something*—then I could protect myself next time. I wouldn't make the same mistake again.

I wouldn't choose the wrong person.

A flurry of pings emanate from my computer, and I remember all final checks need to happen today for Issue 137 of *Hot!* to go to the printers. Chloe's photo had sent my usually relentlessly efficient mind down another direction.

No. It's final proof day. Don't stress. I've gotta work. Let's talk after 9? I text back.

I'm stressing, of course.

Not about the same thing that Chloe is stressing about. My fears are from a different place entirely. But one thing at a time. Right now, I need to get this magazine to the printer. Then I'll tackle Chloe and Kingston and what the fuck to do about that.

But of course Ben ignores me.

He sticks his head around my door twenty minutes later, his handsome brow furrowed, his eyes dark.

Outside, the office has gone quiet, and I think about the hot mess we used to cause in this office. Back when we were younger. When I worried less. I can almost hear a collective sigh of relief from my staff as Ben and I talk in our normal voices—no shouting. No sounds of breakage. I blush slightly at the memory. What on earth were we thinking?

"What are you thinking about?" Ben asks softly, his face smoothing out, becoming less worried, more predatory. More intense.

"Nothing," I mutter, dropping my eyes, my blush mounting.

He grins wickedly. "You're thinking about how quiet everything went when I walked in." He moves closer to me, placing a fingertip underneath my chin, forcing my eyes back up to his.

"And you're remembering why." His eyes don't leave mine for a second, but I brush his hand away, flinching at the memory, ducking to escape those eyes.

"It's in the past," I say huskily, but he runs his fingers slowly along the edge of the desk. The edge I've clung to so many times, hopeless with desire, my legs buckling beneath me, his hands, his tongue...

"You're thinking about it," he whispers, moving behind me, his lips warm and soft against my neck, his hands reaching down and skimming across my hips, the warmth of his breath leaving my lips parted, my breathing shallow. His teeth find my earlobe and tug on it gently. A moan escapes my lips. Everything inside me wants to open my neck up to him, lean back into him, feel his hands wander leisurely across my body, my breasts. As though he has all the time in the world. As though I'm his.

But I pull away, trying to calm my breathing.

His arms fall to his side and I can feel him standing behind me. Sagging a little. *No!* I think immediately, my body desperate for his touch.

"I miss it, too," he says, but he keeps his hands off me. *Thank God* is my next thought, my sensible brain kicking in. Because I don't think I would have the resolve to move away twice.

Finally he moves to the chair opposite me, his eyes dark with lust, his jeans bulging appreciatively. I avert my eyes, my cunt throbbing with longing. It's only been a few weeks, but it might as well have been twenty years, I want him so badly.

"It's probably going to come out, Ada. Judging by that last letter." He watches me carefully. "Will it really be that bad?"

Though I immediately snap, "Yes!" and glare at Ben, the question lingers in my mind.

Mum is all about appearances. She and Bill live outside the city, lording over their small country community, Mum insisting on being on all the committees. Even the local primary school, for God's sake. "My grandchildren will probably go here," she tells people smugly. "My children are high flyers. They won't be in a position to do the day-to-day stuff with raising children."

She says it in front of me, yet has never asked me if I want children, if I'd want to stay at home with them if I do have them, or if I would see her as a suitable candidate to care for them (*expose them to*, I think to myself, seething) if I continued to work.

She never even asks if I'm seeing anyone.

Nor has she seriously considered, obviously, how they might hinder her life of self-important self-indulgence. It'd be hard to flit about—dictating to the book club what books they'll be reading and dominating the conversation—with little people needing her care and attention.

And Chloe. Good lord. Could Mum be more insensitive?

"Why is it so bad?" Ben is looking at me with genuine interest, and I feel a flash of rage toward him.

"We've talked about this. Do you ever pay attention?"

That is grossly unfair, as Ben does in fact pay more attention than anyone I've ever met. It's just another one of the million qualities that make him astonishing and make this whole situation completely fucked. I feel *angry* with him for being so goddamn divine.

"Yes. But I don't think I believe you, actually." Ben is looking at me coolly, the previous look of sexy adoration completely evaporated.

That's what happens when you're a bitch, I think to myself. But then I think—*Good. That's one way to get rid of him.*

"Your complaint has always been that Janey *doesn't* actually care. That she doesn't even notice what you do or don't do. If you're happy or sad. As long as she can tell people how successful you are, and take all the credit, she doesn't give a flying fuck."

"That's different from doing something socially unacceptable! People would laugh at her. Incest kids! She would hate that!" My voice sounds slightly hysterical. Ben sounds perfectly logical and reasonable by comparison. But does he actually know my mother? Living with her for four years hardly counts. Especially when she did her best to ignore the fact that he even existed.

"Has she ever told anyone who you've dated in the last twenty years?"

"Yes. She told everyone about Kingston. How rich and handsome he was." I stare at him stubbornly.

His demeanour shifts. Concern again. "Yeah. The letter. You must be feeling shaken up."

"About my mother! That's what I'm shaken up about. That Chloe will trot off with that letter and hand it over to her. As though she has anything valuable to add to the situation."

"You know, I've heard Janey tell people on many occasions that, basically, you're far too successful and busy to have a partner. I bet we could get married and she just wouldn't tell anyone. We hardly move in the same circles, except for family events. And no one else would care. I mean—Aunt Kate," he pauses and laughs, "she'd just be happy her family weren't the most fucked up. But everyone else couldn't care less. Even Janey —I really don't see her flipping her lid about this, Ada." His tone softens, and he stands up, starts coming back around my desk, but I hold up a hand.

Reluctantly, he sits back down.

"Maybe we should consider it a sign. That we can hook the hell up and bang like bunnies." He grins. Then his face falls, a pained kind of yearning etching across it. "I want that, Ada. I want that so much. And I think you want it too."

My heart free-falls in my chest. That is exactly what I want. And also to smooth away that pain in Ben's eyes. Let myself get lost in his humour and goodness and body.

But I drag my mind elsewhere. Because even the fear of Mum finding out can't compete with the other problems I need to solve right now.

Firstly—how can I trust myself to choose the right man after such a goddamn disaster?

And secondly, while everyone else panics about whether we're in danger, I need to work out—if Kingston isn't sending these letters...then who the fuck is?

19

ADA – 33 YEARS OLD

APRIL 2014

"He asked me to marry him."

"WHAT?!!" After that initial word, flung from her mouth with unusual thoughtlessness, Chloe is struck silent. She's trying to form words, her mouth literally open, working around a syllable that never comes.

"Is it that crazy?" I say. "He's like my perfect match. Smart, sexy, focussed. He's career-orientated. He has drive. And he wants a family and has been waiting forever."

"To find you?"

She doesn't mean it as a put-down, but her doubts are dancing all over her face.

"You've known him for like, six weeks. You can't know if someone is right for you that quickly. I'm sorry. You just can't. It's crazy."

This is exactly what I've been thinking, but hearing Chloe say it makes me about turn. *Typical*, I think to myself. *She doesn't even ask what I think, just tells me what to think.* It makes me want to really get her worked up.

"Oh, I don't know," I say breezily. "I'm thinking about it. I mean, when it feels so right, why wait? I'm not getting any younger. It's really now or never if I want kids." Chloe stares at me, perplexed.

"You hate kids," she says.

I pretend to bristle. Chloe has never asked me what I think about kids. "That is not true. I just don't think they come out on top in a cost-benefit analysis for return on investment. I like my days to have more measurable success markers."

To my surprise, she actually looks worried rather than angry. Anger is her usual go-to expression when we don't see eye to eye.

"Well, don't make any rash decisions. Think it over a bit longer," she urges me, her conciliatory tone more alarming than any level of her anger. Then, as though an afterthought, ever so casually: "What does Ben think?"

That definitely throws me.

"What do you care what Ben thinks?" I snap. "I would have thought you'd be over the moon if I got hitched to someone else. You've been *quite* clear about that." As much as I try, I can't keep the bitterness out of my voice.

Because whatever I tell myself about "doing the right thing"— if my family had been on board with the idea, I'd have married Ben in a heartbeat.

20

BEN

November 22, 2017

After insisting to Ada that I'd check back in with her later, I sit in a bar two blocks away, nursing a whiskey.

Wondering if Janey has seen the letter. Wondering if Dad has.

Hoping, in a way, that we could just get this over with. I really doubt the fallout will be as spectacular as Ada seems to think it will be.

Maybe, in fact, Kingston has done me a great favour. Pressing all of Chloe's buttons. She'll be a livewire right now. Discretion was never a priority for her. I've wondered how she kept the news of Ada and me to herself for so long, actually. It seemed like just the piece of juicy gossip she'd enjoy sharing with Janey for the short burst of excitement that ensued. Why she kept it to herself all these years remains a mystery.

And also offers me a glimmer of hope.

If she really disapproved and it was really such a big deal, surely the quickest way to get me out of Ada's bed was to blow the affair open. Bring Ada back in line. And though she avoids confrontation, surely she could have set it up so she wasn't seen as tattling. Sent an "accidental" email. Made a slip.

The more that I sit here and think about it, the crazier the whole situation seems.

Ada loves me.

Does she really need her mother's approval more?

Her mother has never given two bloody shits about anything except herself. It's almost pitiful, the way Ada needs Janey's approval. Like she's stuck in some parent-child dynamic because she never got the affirmation as a child that other children get. So there she stays. Chasing. Hoping. Longing.

On the outside, our family looks so fucking perfect.

Wealthy. Successful.

Dad, at least, is genuinely an extraordinarily good guy. Chloe, Ada, and I are all at the top of our fields.

Funny how murky it gets when you look under the surface.

Does Janey really care about what's underneath? Or as long as the superficial stuff presents the right image, does it not really matter? She looks like a good mother. She's fun and physically present and makes sure we all catch up regularly. Being truly interested, taking the time to really see Ada as she really is— that's apparently much less important to her. Or maybe she just has no idea how to do that.

But Chloe? Chloe always seems like she's competing with Ada. To be the good daughter. The successful daughter. The interesting daughter.

What quicker way than to win that battle once and for all than to let it slip that Ada is with me?

Right now, it just doesn't add up.

Sitting with a whiskey, trying to untangle what on earth is going on, I find it hard not to think about the early days.

We'd muddled through university, sneaking around, telling no one about our affair. Ada working at one thousand and ten percent, much like at high school. While I skived off study whenever I could, discovering grungy bands and grungy pubs, cheap Thai takeaway, and a new and extensive group of like-minded mates to goof around with, Ada went to all the classes, plus some extras just for fun, plotting her reading and assignments out on a giant wall calendar hanging in her room.

But we'd end up studying together for long stretches, Ada patiently explaining the things to me that I'd missed in classes that we shared, rolling her eyes, and sometimes blatantly lying, teaching me rubbish, her face deadpan until my confusion gave way to understanding that she was having me on. And then, invariably—crazy, beautiful sex.

She was the highlight of my days, my weeks, my life. I was desperate to introduce her to everyone as my girlfriend, but she wouldn't have a bar of it.

"Your dad will adore you no matter what you do," she grumbled once, frowning. "My mother's love is kind of conditional: *'Be pretty. Be accomplished. Be the envy of the crowd. Only bend the rules if they help you to achieve these things.'* This. Us. Can't you see how fucked up this is?"

"No," I had replied.

Even on top of not thinking being stepsiblings mattered so much, I didn't understand why Ada cared so much. Janey seemed to play about as much a part in her life as pursuing pleasure did.

Zilch.

I indicate to the barman that I'd like a refill, my mind full of Ada and all the reasons I want her to be mine.

"I'm going to start a magazine," she'd told me one day when we were barely out of university. She was deadly serious, twirling her hair around her pen in the way that she did when she was concentrating hard.

I was surprised for a moment, but then not really. Why not? Ada had the skills and the drive to do whatever the hell she wanted.

"Oh, yeah?" I had said. "What about?"

"Sex," she'd replied, and my jaw had dropped.

And she'd grinned at me in that way she had, half joyful, half sex-goddess.

She'd done it, too. Made a little magazine that sold sex. Celebrity gossip stories, of course. But in there she weaved women's stories with a rawness and honesty that had won her an enormous following. Just the right mix of smart and sexy. And her little magazine turned into a bigger magazine and then a giant magazine. Fifteen years later, she was still at the peak of her game.

My own rise to the top of a rival magazine was the complete opposite of hers: a joking internship to compare notes with her; a surprising and previously unknown knack for leading a team and bringing out the best in people; the commerce know-how to succeed, despite our product being the shabbier version of Ada's.

So then we were competitors, printing similar stories at least when it came to celebrity gossip and sexy themes. I was always the first to admit that *Hot!* published more meaningful stuff amongst the rubbish.

And as competitors, Ada invented my favourite game.

I down my whiskey. Just thinking about the game makes my cock twitch in my pants.

The rules were simple.

We played in Ada's office only. She would call me over to "discuss" something when we had a professional dispute... usually feigning rage.

The discussion would be fucking, behind her closed doors.

Whoever gasped or moaned out loud had to remove an item of clothing of the other's choice.

Whoever came first, lost.

Whoever won got to choose how whatever problem we were discussing would be resolved.

If anyone in either office found out, the game would be over, forever.

Usually, Ada won. But really, was anyone a loser in this game? If you lost, you still came. It was basically a win-win, in my opinion. Maybe even a win-win-win. Because the game itself was one helluva way to spend an afternoon.

I slap a twenty on the bar and nod to the barman.

Then I head out to get at least one of my questions answered from the source.

21

BEN – 28 YEARS OLD

MAY 2008

I'm grinning like a fool.

Bright sunlight is glancing off all the other rich people's offices overlooking the botanical gardens on St Kilda Road. Autumn colours are creeping across the bright, well-watered greens. The Yarra twinkles in the distance.

This day, suddenly, is looking brilliant.

On my Mac is the draft copy of an interview with Julia Roberts about her career with a baby. The copy is from *Hot!*, obtained by one of my interns from one of Ada's. It wasn't even my idea, though Ada will find that hard to believe.

Whatever. She'll be mad as hell. At least on the outside.

If anyone barged into my office now—I'm Acting CEO for a month, while Delaney is away, twirling in his $2000 chair—they'd misinterpret my glee. They'd think I'm grinning like the cat that got the cream because we can use this information to undermine *Hot!* Get something better. Hotter. Or do a quick, probably substandard article on Julia to run at the same time, so readers will never know who had the story first, who was the copycat. No matter what Ada says on Twitter about it, doubt will prevail.

Let them think that.

But that's not why I'm smiling.

I'm smiling because Ada is going to call me.

And she's going to want to play my favourite game.

RIGHT ON CUE, my phone buzzes.

Ada.

"Hey there, little sister," I murmur into the phone, my tone soft and warm. Loving, even. Because God, I love this woman.

"Hey there, little brother," she replies in kind. It's the only sentence she'll utter that is soft and inviting. Acknowledging that this here, this isn't really as serious as she'll shortly make it sound.

Technically, Ada is the little sister—by a whole four days, as I love to remind her. So our greeting is an ongoing private joke. That Ada always considers herself older, wiser, and one step ahead. But she loves me just as much. She doesn't declare it the way that I do. But I can feel it, see it. Bathe in it.

You can't spend ten-odd years together—however secret we might keep it—and be this close without love coming into the equation.

"You stole our copy."

Ada's voice switches easily to hard and accusing. I can almost see her flinty stare. I feel my cock twitch in my jeans.

"No stealing involved," I reply smoothly. "One of our interns just called and asked for it. Stupid ploy, of course. And no one on the books here approved it. She did it off her own bat and in her own time. And someone at your end chose to send it to her. Seems more a case of stupidity on your end than criminality on ours." I keep my voice honey-like, dripping with niceties, though I'm quite proud of the little barb about stupidity.

"Regardless of the intern's stupidity,"—Ada clarifies sharply where the blame lies—"the plan from your end was deception. To deceive us and gain intel by playing on someone's naiveté. Not playing nice, Ben," she tsk-tsks over the phone, her tone now like a school mistress.

Like there might need to be some punishment involved.

"I think you might be jealous, sis," I say, knowing the familiarity will rile her. "We are obviously better at selecting our interns. Better perception, maybe. Or better interview questions. Ours somehow end up autonomous and inventive while yours seem a little too...*innocent* for this field."

I let my mouth hover around the word *innocent*, drawing out the sound. I know Ada will pick up on this. That she'll now be thinking about how innocent we're not.

I know her so well.

But then, the reverse is also true.

"I want it back. All the emails deleted. All hard copies shredded. And I want you over here now so I can delete it from your mind."

"Impossible, Ada," I sigh in false sorrow. "I've got too many meetings today. And also, how will you delete it from my mind? I've already been putting those words to images in my head. The pictures must be stunning. Such a cute age. Such a beautiful mum. Any breastfeeding ones?" I add, innocently.

"*Do as you're told,*" Ada hisses. "Come. Here. Right. Now."

Yes, she knows me well. She knows I love her being commanding. She knows I love this bloody game. She knows that I'll come, no matter what I'm in the middle of doing.

Because she knows that I'm semi-hard already.

WHEN I ENTER the offices of *Hot!*, silence descends.

It's not just that I'm the enemy, trying all sorts of wily ways to undermine and outdo them. Their dislike isn't loyalty to their magazine; it's loyalty to their paycheck. Magazines are transient: here one minute, gone the next. I've lost count of how many competitors have gone under over the last few years. So they basically don't want me to win because they might end up out of a job.

I tease Ada that it's also because I'm not so bad to look at myself, throwing back at her all the things I know she loves about me. Shaggy, just-got-out-of-pleasing-you-in-bed hair. Sexy grin, languid charm. "My boy-next-door good looks scream sex, you know," I've smirked in the past, the compliment paid to me by her, many years ago. Stored up with all the other ones.

"Yesssss," she'd responded, pretending not to be amused or flattered that I remembered. "You look like the type of womaniser who'd have you up against the wall with your legs spread in five seconds flat."

I'd smiled at her wickedly and put her in that exact position, just like that.

But no, it was none of these things.

The silence fell because of how Ada would react. My visits meant conflict: shouting, anger. Breakages, even.

Tension in the office while everyone waited for an outcome.

Though by the time I leave, Ada is always in a damn fine mood.

ADA IS LEANING against her doorframe as I saunter up.

Her hair is tied into a fierce bun, her perfect heart-shaped face and sculpted cheekbones clearly delineated. Her full, red lips are pressed together into a tight line. Her almond eyes are sharp. Her breasts are heaving in mock rage underneath her white shirt.

Her mock rage is very convincing. The first time, I'd been terrified. I couldn't actually remember Ada ever being truly angry with me. But she had ushered me inside and hit play on something on her computer.

Raised voices—mainly hers. Some shouting. Some throwing of things.

I had stared at her in confusion.

"I've tested it all," she'd smiled reassuringly. "It's at just the right volume for what I have in mind. If you stick to my rules."

She'd then gone on to explain the whole thing. I'd nearly died between the desire and the terror. Given how worried she was about people finding out, wasn't this a little risky?

"That's part of the fun," she had smiled, lazily raising her skirt and sliding her hand between her legs.

She'd won in about three minutes flat that time.

Now, she pushes herself off the doorframe deliberately slowly. She's wearing a knee-length black skirt, which hugs her very enticing butt and thighs. My eyes roam over it appreciatively, imagining it scrunched up around her waist. My cock twitches again at the thought.

My eyes travel back up to hers, which are narrowed and blazing.

"We have a problem to work out, Mr. Farris," she says icily.

Involuntarily, staff all across the floor cringe or wince. Her tone is terrifying.

I don't wince though.

I saunter into her room feeling pretty fucking fabulous indeed.

As soon as the door is closed and locked behind me, I swing around, grab Ada by the hips, and push her back up against the door we've just walked through, wedging one leg between hers and moving my hands across her arse.

It is the goddamn bomb, this arse.

Burying my lips in her neck, I let out an involuntary groan.

Ada grins triumphantly.

"Pants," she says, and I roll my eyes. She always trumps me at this part of the game. Not that I care. I like shedding my clothes, being naked near Ada.

And I don't mind her remaining dressed, clothes bunched around her ankles or hoisted up to her waist. She looks so fucking *taken* that way. Which is all part of the game we're playing.

I yank my pants—and what the hell, shoes too—off as she hits play on her arguing-with-Ben soundtrack. Then we circle each other warily, sizing each other up. I think I know all of Ada's tricks. A favourite sneaky manoeuvre of hers is a finger up my asshole. At the right moment, I completely lose control.

Her voice can also be deadly: telling me how hard or how deep to fuck her in just the right tone—desperate, beside herself, wanting me so badly. It's intoxicating. She's perfected it over the years.

"You've been a bad boy, Mr. Farris," she murmurs, sultry and seductive, one finger tracing her nipple over her shirt. "I think you need to be punished," she goes on, running her tongue along her upper lip. I groan again before I even register what's happening.

Ada grins again.

"Shirt," she says, and as I tug it over my head, she eyes my pecs appreciatively.

God, what this woman does to me.

"Hands on the desk, Mr. Farris," she murmurs, leading me to her desk by the waist of my Calvin Kleins, glancing over her shoulder at me, pouty centrefold girl. She must have practiced that look too, damn her. Then she walks around behind me and adjusts the spread of my feet with her own.

She traces one finger across my butt, murmuring, "How

would you like to do me today, Mr. Farris? Over the desk, maybe? Or maybe you'd like to put that gorgeous, hard cock up my arse?"

I groan again.

"God, you're easy today," Ada mutters, then is straight back into the role play. "Briefs," she says, and I'm now butt naked except for my socks, my cock jutting out enthusiastically to greet her. I turn to face her, and she sighs and reaches for it, lust clouding her eyes. Her touch is electric, and I pull her into me and kiss her deeply, one hand on her arse, the other fondling a breast through her clothes. I can feel her nipple harden beneath my touch, and she arches into me, but she doesn't make a sound.

She's stroking the length of my cock slow and firm, the other hand moving down to gently cup my balls. Trying to keep the surprise edge, I roughly spin her around and put her hands on the desk, covering them with mine, pinning her in place. Kissing her neck and shoulders, nibbling at her gently, pushing her legs apart with my knee, I want to take her now—fuck this game. But I try to remember how good waiting is. With one hand I start to tug her skirt up over the curve of her magnificent ass.

Moving quickly, I push my fingers under the lace of her underwear and slide them slowly along her lips.

"Christ, you're wet," I mutter, one finger slowly pushing inside her. I can smell her already. She smells like heaven.

Breathing deeply, I pull back from her and peel her underpants down her legs, tracing kisses down her calves, admiring the shape of them as she obligingly steps out of them. She's still wearing her black strappy heels, and the sight of her legs in heels with her bare arse in the air is nearly more than I can bear. Then she starts moving her arse from side to side.

"Oh Ben," she fake moans, "Stick it in me. Stick your big, hard cock in there. In my wet, tight, hot little pussy. Fuck me hard, baby. Pump me so good."

I slap her ass, grinning.

"Don't tempt me," I growl, then drop to my knees and lick her slit.

This time, Ada moans.

"Shirt," I command breathlessly from between her thighs. Then I keep licking. Ada groans again before she can stop herself.

"Bra," I say between long, slow licks.

"Help me," Ada says—another ploy—but I stand behind her anyway, undoing one button at a time, slowly peeling the shirt off her milky shoulders. It's like unwrapping the present you never thought you'd ever get, no matter how many times someone assures you that they bought you that very thing you always wanted.

I unclip her bra and her tits swing free. They're glorious—large and firm and delicious. I reach around and squeeze them hungrily. Then I stand back to admire my handiwork. Her arse is in the air in front of me, skirt bunched around her waist like she wants me so bad there was no time to undress.

And the shoes. *God.*

I love a woman in heels.

This woman.

This woman in heels.

Her legs are spread in front of me. She's leaning over the desk like she's mine for the taking. That I can do whatever I want with that arse, that pussy.

My cock is aching. I could probably stroke myself a couple of times and come all over her arse, watch my cum drip down her legs and onto the floor of her oh-so-professional office. I nearly come just thinking about it.

But Ada, with a little breathing space to collect her thoughts, whips around and drops to her knees in front of me. Her skirt is still scrunched up around her waist. Her tits jut proudly out from her chest, her nipples hard and pink. She's looking up at me through her eyelashes, licking her lips. She looks so fucking hot.

"You want me to suck you?" she says. "Lick that big, hot cock till you're moaning with pleasure? Filling my mouth?"

I close my eyes, managing to stop the groan that is rising in my throat. Not that losing my socks is going to give Ada any advantage.

I nod, thinking it will be the end of me.

Ada takes my cock in her mouth, swirls her tongue around my head then runs it down the ridge of skin along the length of me. My cock flexes and strains in response. Then she takes me into her mouth deeply, sucking gently, her tongue moving ceaselessly. I can't help it—I groan. But knowing she has the advantage, Ada doesn't stop blowing me to tell me to take my socks off. Her hands are creeping up my legs. One hand cups my balls, squeezing gently. The other hand starts making its way around my butt.

I catch her hands in mine and step away from her, my cock bereft at the loss of her warm, wet mouth.

"Nice try, lady. Now on your feet."

Ada smiles at me slowly. I never know if she'll obey me or not. I don't really care. Whatever path this game takes, it's always thirty-five stars out of ten. I've never had hotter sex in my life.

But this time, she does obey.

"What next, big brother?" she says mockingly, her eyes on my dick. Then she licks her lips slowly and leans back on the desk, reaching one hand down to her slit. She starts slowly circling her clit. Then she pushes two fingers inside herself.

I groan again.

"You owe me two items. And you've only got one," she says slowly. "Let me think....hmmm. I think I get a command as well," she says. "What do you think?"

"Sure," I reply, my eyes still on her fingers moving languidly in and out of her cunt.

"Socks. And then bend over the desk."

I oblige.

"Spread them," she says, and I spread my legs, my cock rock hard, my balls aching.

"I need to fuck you soon," I mutter, thinking I really can't take much more if she wants this to end with my cock inside her, rather than a giant mess all over her desk.

"Soon," she shushes me, planting a kiss on my shoulder. Then she drops to her knees behind me.

"Oh god," I moan, and she spreads my butt cheeks wide. Then her tongue is circling my butthole. It's warm and wet and so fucking hot. Jesus Christ. I moan again. I don't care about the game anymore. Just Ada. Her tongue. Her fingers. Her perfect, hot little slit.

She licks, explores, but I need to be inside her. Now. Hard. Standing up, I spin around, grab her arms and pull her upright, guiding her to face the window, pressing her hands against the glass. Then I spread her legs with my knee, turn her head and kiss her once, deep and urgent, my tongue everywhere in her mouth, my need insatiable. Then I guide my cock into her slit.

"Take it," I gasp and thrust into her, buckling at the knees to get the angle right, my cock sliding in as though it belongs there, like there's nothing else. I hold still for a moment, my cock as far in as I can push it, my forehead against her shoulder, one hand pulling her hair free.

"Tell Melbourne how much you love my cock," I whisper in her ear.

"Ben. Cock," Ada pants. She can't even form sentences. She wants me now too. Hard, fast, calling the shots.

"Hard. The best," she moans, trying to push back into me, feel me further, deeper inside her. Get more of me. All of me.

I groan into her hair. "You destroy me," I mutter. Then I grab her hips and yank her arse backwards, so she's bent at the waist, her hands sliding down the glass, her breath forming fog on the window.

Then I fuck her like my life depends on it.

My hands grip her hips, pulling her into me every thrust, moaning her name each time I ram in. "Ada. Fuck. Ada."

Ada arches her back, moaning my name, pushing off the glass for even deeper penetration, meeting me at each thrust, the rhythm perfect, her desire spiralling my need higher, higher, higher.

I reach around to grab a handful of tit. I love feeling them shudder with each thrust of my cock. There's so much of her that is delicious, my hands don't know where to start or stop.

Reflected in the glass, I can see her bouncing tits, her open, gasping mouth. I'm panting and grunting, completely lost in her, in this moment. I reach around to rub her clit, my fingers moving fast, our breathing ragged. She's close, too. I can hear it in her breathing, her whimpers, the way her breath catches in her throat.

I look down at my cock sliding in and out of her. It's wet and slick and glorious. I can see her heels on either side of it. Her legs, spread for me. Her cunt, taking me. Her, against the window, wanting me.

"Do you like that, little sister?" I whisper hoarsely. "Do you like my cock sliding in so deep? Do you like it rammed up there so far while you look out the window? Fucking you so hard?"

"Yes" is all Ada can manage between gasps. Then: "More."

More cock or more words, I don't care. I can give both.

"I love the feel of your tight little cunt, clutching my cock, hungry for it. I love how wet you get for me. Do you get this wet for anyone else, Ada? Or just me?"

"Just you," Ada gasps. "Don't stop."

"I'm going to ram it up here so good, all of Melbourne is going to hear you come," I whisper, my fingers frantic at her clit, thrusting my cock urgently inside her. "They'll look up at your posh office and wonder what could possibly be so good up here at 11 a.m. on a Monday morning." My voice is raspy, my need and my love for this woman overwhelming me. Wet, thrusting sex sounds punctuate my words. "Then they'll see your hands spread on the window and know you're getting some good, deep cock, you dirty little girl."

Then Ada is coming, thrusting back against me, arching her back, crying out, her cunt clenching my cock in delicious waves, and I'm coming too, my cock pulsing and flexing inside her, my lips moaning in her hair, my hands finding her tits, her lips, her hips, grinding and grabbing because I can't get enough of her. I can be coming inside her with my hands full of her and I already want more of her. She's like a drug, and I don't know which bit to taste first or most or hardest.

We stand like this, me still thrusting gently, her insides still clutching my cock, breathing heavily. Ada collapses against me, my arms around her holding her up.

Holding her tenderly.

I kiss the nape of her neck—gentle, quiet kisses. My love and wonder rolling out of me and filling the whole room.

Eventually I help her find her feet and she moves to the desk, grabs a handful of tissues. Offers the box to me, smiling. Satisfied.

We get dressed in silence. Ada recaptures her hair in its stern bun. She reapplies her lipstick with deft strokes.

Within minutes, we look each other up and down, smooth each other's clothes, wipe stray hairs from unlikely places.

We grin briefly at each other.

"I love you," I tell her, and she leans forward, closes her eyes, presses her lips to mine, almost as though she's in pain.

"I win," she says.

Then she pauses the recording at an appropriate place, calls up a severe frown, and walks me to the door.

22

ADA

November 23, 2017

"Earth to Ada, earth to Ada." Jase clicks his fingers in front of my face and I snap back to the here and now.

"You going to tell me what's going on? Not like you to daydream. Issue 137 went to the printers yesterday. You're usually halfway through the next one by now, prodding us all into action. No time to celebrate! The work must go on!" His tone is teasing, but we have had heated discussions about giving the team an easy day after we wrap up an issue. I can't imagine why anyone would want to sit around the office chatting and eating cake when they could get stuck into the next project.

"Yes, but not everyone is quite as obsessive as you. And other people find self-worth in things other than what they achieve. Like, the quality of their relationships," he'd said.

That conversation had been less teasing. But after this many years together, Jason has learnt that I work best—and the magazine soars—when I do it my way. And he can take it or leave it.

So far, he's taken it.

I consider him carefully. Usually, I would talk to him about this. But I feel twitchy. Despite hours and hours of thinking, I've pretty much gone round and round in circles. And it's making me paranoid. I've thought of everyone. Even Jason. Could Jason be sending the letters? Trying to freak me out? Because he's actually an ambitious, deceitful turd who wants to scare me out of my job?

But not even Jason knows about Ben and me. Only Chloe knows. At least, I think only Chloe knows. And Chloe is too hysterical to be sending letters. Even with a motive, she couldn't fake it this much, could she? And so far, I can't think of a motive. What does she have to gain from sending letters and pretending they're from Kingston? Jason at least might get my job for a while if I am scared into hiding.

But I can't shake the thought that she and Trevor bought that house after Kingston and I broke up. They're silent electors. They're not in the phone book. There is no possible way Kingston could know where she lives to leave a letter there...is there?

And as I ponder this some more, the little nagging worry that has wormed its way into my mind starts taking a clearer shape. Forming a sentence.

That being: *Chloe might actually like Mum to find out about Ben and me.*

23

ADA – 16 YEARS OLD

OCTOBER *1996*

"Ada threw all of Shirleen's lunch in the rubbish bin today, Mum!" Chloe informed Mum over dinner in a singsong voice, joyful over my transgression, my impulsiveness, my lack of control.

Mum didn't seem to hear her, continuing on with her crossword, not taking her eyes from it even as she took bites of the slice of pizza hanging from one hand.

"She had DETENTION!!" Chloe shouted.

Mum had raised her eyebrows at me at that. I'd managed to get to sixteen without a single detention. So I suppose that was kind of worthy of an eyebrow raise.

She hadn't looked cross, but Mum being cross was not what I was worried about.

But I needn't have worried; she was not interested in the details. She asked why—"she was being horrible" was all I told her—then suggested it would be wise not to do such a thing again.

Then she went back to her crossword.

Later, it's Chloe's divulgence of that information that sticks with me. Her glee to have Mum see me as "bad" or "impulsive." I had explained what had happened to her in confidence on the way home, thinking she might comfort me, or at least just listen to my confusion—and she did, at the time.

Shirleen wasn't even a friend. But she was popular and pretty, and had invited me to sit with her at lunch. I didn't even care that much; it wasn't like I didn't have my own friends. But everyone seemed to adore Shirleen, so I thought, *cool, new friend.*

And she never showed up, and apparently was watching, laughing with her friends, as I sat alone where she had told me to meet her, confused.

Emma had told me later, when I gave up and went back to sit with her and our girl gang. And I'd been so pissed off. Humiliated, embarrassed—but also angry. Who does that sort of shit? It's like bloody preschool.

So I had marched over, grabbed her lunchbox, and dumped the whole thing in the nearest bin.

It wasn't even that I was that upset about it. Confused, mostly. I wasn't the girl that was bullied. There were many others who had been cursed with that role. I was confused about why suddenly Shirleen had wanted to pick on me, and confused about the torrent of feelings I had had in response.

But that night, I lay in bed and stared at the ceiling, confused about Chloe's behaviour. Her initial rage at Shirleen, the protective older sister. She had made me feel okay about what happened and how I felt. But then, at dinner, she wanted me to relive it?

She served it up like a funny anecdote from the day for Mum's entertainment, completely indifferent about the feelings I had expressed to her earlier.

What the fuck?

Didn't she know how Mum's lack of interest in the things that mattered to me felt? Did she experience her so differently? Because it seemed that Chloe should understand that very well.

Mum was equally disinterested in Chloe. At least, that's the way it seemed to me.

As I lay there thinking about it that night, another thought occurred to me.

Maybe it was not for entertainment. Maybe it was meaner than that.

Maybe what Chloe actually wanted was for Mum to see me humiliated or in the wrong.

Does she want *Mum to think poorly of me?* I had wondered for the first time that day.

But it wouldn't be the last time I wondered that. And it wouldn't be long before I stopped telling Chloe any of my secrets, anything close to my soul.

So when the magical, magnetic, tsunami-like torrent of thoughts and feelings about Ben moved into an actual, physical, glorious thing, I kept that secret far, far away from her untrustworthy grasp.

24

ADA

NOVEMBER 23, 2017

"NO! It's still not right."

Jase is rubbing his temple, eyes closed, his frustration barely under control.

It's nearly 10 p.m. and he wants to go home. I've urged him to do so; that I prefer finalising things myself, anyway. But he's refusing to leave me here until this is signed off on.

"If I leave you, you'll be here all night to change one word and you'll be a fucking nightmare to all the staff tomorrow!" he snaps.

"I'm never a nightmare," I respond, genuinely confused. I always take such care to be polite, even though it nearly kills me.

"Ada. You look at people as though they're imbeciles. You talk to them slowly and in a kind but fake voice...as though they're imbeciles. You try to hide the fact that you think everyone is...an imbecile. You make people feel like shit."

I look at him in surprise.

"I thought I hid it better than that," I mutter.

Finally he puts his hands in his pockets and takes a deep breath. I can see he's trying to deal with me in a way that doesn't make his head explode. What he doesn't realise is that he's wasting his time. I don't care. I'll do it my way, just like I have for the last fifteen years. Whether he conveys his opinion with his head exploding or with the forced calmness he is trying desperately to convey.

"We've been over this section all afternoon. And we only just filed the last issue. We have *weeks* to look at this. This is getting insane, Adds. Have you ever heard of the saying 'Perfect is the enemy of good'? This is *good*. It's not worth spending three more hours on to take it from 99% good to 100% perfect. We can't function this way. Everyone is exhausted. Everyone is sick of working like this. You can't expect your entire staff to deliver perfect, 100% of the time. It's just not real life."

"I don't expect them to. That's why I'm here, fixing it up. They do the legwork. I make it perfect."

"You're not supposed to!" he shouts, the head explosion winning, finally. "You're the goddamn CEO! You're supposed to steer the overall creative direction! The finances! The staff! You're not supposed to obsess over whether to use the word *wonderful* or *beautiful* for three hours! And you're *certainly* not supposed to make the staff feel crappy if they make little mistakes! *Everyone* makes mistakes." He looks at me meaningfully.

"Everyone should try harder," I snap.

"Really? Really, Ada? Have you never really made a mistake? Had to have other people mop up after you?" He's cocking his head at me, skirting dangerously close to The Thing We Never Talk About. And even though on one level, I know he's only raising it to make a point, I also feel sick with disbelief.

"Well, maybe that's part of why I am trying so hard, Jason," I say, cocking my head right back at him, my voice betraying no hint of the emotion raging beneath it.

The feeling of being sucker-punched.

"But I have to say I'm disappointed in you for bringing it up. Now get the fuck out of my office and let me make my own big-girl decisions about how I run my own business. When you're in charge, then you can do it however the fuck you like."

I turn back to my computer, the picture of icy but poised, and wait for him to leave.

"Shut the door behind you, *please*," I say, reinforcing his point, but I don't care.

That's as close as anyone (*besides Chloe*, I think, and realise that I quickly follow that with *but she doesn't count*) has ever come to throwing Kingston in my face. The mistake that keeps on giving, it seems.

Somehow it was conveyed as a taboo subject, without me ever saying a word. But Jason, security, my PA, tech support—they all made adjustments to take care of business post-Kingston without anyone murmuring the words that were on my own lips every other moment.

How the fuck did you end up with this guy, Adds?

What the fuck were you thinking?

And the thing that really bugs me the most: in a life dictated by doing everything "right"—the sacrifices, the shabby social life, the shitty dinners, the hours of study, the lack of fun—doing "daughter" right, "student" right, "sister" right—all to get this bloody perfect life making my perfect magazine, doing exactly what I love—so many checks and balances, so many lists and checkboxes—*how did I choose someone so motherfucking wrong?*

And from there, it's not much of a jump to—if I can be so blind and have such poor judgement when it comes to choosing *one* person, how can I trust myself to choose another?

If I worked that hard to do everything right, and still got it so wrong, maybe it's not possible to do better?

Because the one thing I've always trusted is my own judgement. My mind. My ability to read people and situations and business opportunities—everything. I look and assess and get it right.

Except with Kingston.

And if I can get it wrong once, how can I be sure I won't get it wrong again?

25

ADA – 33 YEARS OLD

APRIL 2014

Kingston swept into my life and stole my heart.

Just like a fucking fairy tale.

Six weeks of romantic bliss. Nice meals, open conversations, so much in common. Best of all, I didn't have to hide it. People asked what I was doing that evening and my heart didn't lurch.

"I'm seeing a movie with my boyfriend," I'd say, without a second thought.

A skiing holiday in Japan—the first holiday I'd taken from the magazine in about five years.

"I'm rich," he'd said, laughing and shrugging. Surprising me with the tickets.

A dazzling week of snow, onsens, food, and sex.

My girlfriends started to complain that they never saw me anymore. They barely saw me anyway—now it was impossible.

I finally found a night to squeeze them in between King—and yes, I was calling him that by then—and work, sharing a bottle of champagne in a little French restaurant just out of town.

"So how was Japan?" Madeline had asked, wiggling her eyebrows at me.

I'd barely had a chance to answer—we were not even through our entrees—when he showed up. A look I couldn't quite decipher passed across his face as he stood in the doorway, before he had seen me. But as soon as our eyes met he grinned broadly, waved and weaved his way through the closely spaced tables to ours. The girls looked at me quizzically, annoyance clear on their faces. I was embarrassed.

"I missed you," he said, his intense hazel eyes fastening on mine. His arm came around my waist when I stood up to greet him. It was gentle, loving. Possessive. I decided it wasn't *that* weird, though there were many interesting glances exchanged around the table that night, too.

"And I wanted to meet your friends." He beamed around at them, charming, attentive. Whatever reservations they had about his intrusion, he soon won them over with his thoughtful conversation, the way he remembered little details about their lives.

"Oh, yes! Ada mentioned you were into cycling! You rode *how many* kilometres this morning?"

They were eating out of his hand by the end of the night. We strolled home, hand in hand, and I was pleased he had come out to find me. I felt enveloped in love and warmth and the rightness of it all. At the time, it felt like I had found my perfect match: we liked all the same things, we were both confident and passionate, he seemed so open and honest. And that body. Good God. For a man who never seemed to exercise at all, he was built like a Greek god.

But looking back, it was mostly—perhaps wholly—that he wasn't my stepbrother.

The dirty little secret that had plagued me for a decade and a half looked set to be put to rest. And no one need be any the wiser.

I lapped up his attention like the fool that I was.

26

ADA

November 23, 2017

Back in my apartment, I slam another bowl of dhal onto my table.

My neat, little, dark hardwood table, always scrupulously bare, handmade for two.

Because I don't entertain. I don't have people over. I'm too busy achieving things. So much a given that I even chose a table to reflect my intentions.

Me and a frozen meal.

And occasionally my lover.

Thinking about Ben nearly winds me, my longing is so intense. He'd make me laugh about my fight with Jason. Without even meaning to, he'd provide me with the line or the angle that would make it okay, give me the idea or the motivation to fix it. Somehow make me feel loveable and adorable rather than like a failure.

An unsettling cloud of something settles over me. I can't even pinpoint what exactly it is. Kingston. Failure. It permeates my whole being, not so much a thought as a feeling.

Wrong wrong wrong wrong wrong runs on replay in my head,

and I can't form clearer sentences about it. My mind veers away from it and toward Ben, because he is comfort and warmth and love.

Because he would make me feel better.

But Ben is so tangled up in this mistake. He motivated it. Now he's being threatened to be exposed by it. Not that he cares. Because mostly, mostly, he wants to be with me. But how can I be sure that I will ever make a good decision about men ever again?

Kingston seemed like everything, but he was not.

Ben seems like everything, but he's my stepbrother.

You've known him forever, I argue with myself. *It would be impossible to know someone for that long and misjudge them. IMPOSSIBLE.*

I think about calling Chloe or Mum instead, but the sinking feeling that accompanies the thought gives me the answer to that idea. Chloe would try to help, but somehow end up intensifying the feelings of guilt for dragging her into this mess.

And Mum? Well, she'd just inadvertently remind me how little I matter. How my concerns and feelings are nothing to her. But oh, did she tell me about the conversation she led at book club last week? Everyone felt she had *such* an insightful take on the situation. Someone even suggested she write to the Department of Education about it! That it would be useful to include in their reading notes on the book to help students studying it!

As I shovel dhal into my mouth—purely functional, with none of the enjoyment or satisfaction my well-prepared, time-saving, tasty meals usually offer me—the reality of this makes me start to feel...something.

Alone.

Angry that I can't turn to Mum or Chloe, because they don't know how to help me, even if they felt inclined to.

Angry with myself, because I have pushed Ben away, and he's

the only one who gets me, the only one who'd know how to help and would actually make time to do so.

Tears suddenly prick at my eyes, at the things I've given up. And for what? This shithouse relationship with my mother?

Fuck.

Fuck, fuck, fuck, fuck, fuck.

As I wipe angrily at my tears, something starts to crystallise in front of me. And with it, a horrible free-falling of my stomach.

That perhaps Kingston isn't the biggest mistake I've made.

I've also prioritised my family—no, not my family. I've prioritised my sister and my mother, who I cannot turn to for support, which is supposed to be the very definition of family!—over Ben and myself.

What they want. What they would approve of. To preserve a relationship that doesn't actually provide me with anything in return.

As opposed to Ben, who's always provided me with absolutely everything I've ever needed. To the point that I know, without a shadow of a doubt, that he would make me feel better right now. That he always knows exactly what I need, even when I can't work it out.

That perhaps Ben is actually my family. The family you get to choose. The family who see who you truly are and love you anyway.

The family that matters.

27

ADA – 34 YEARS OLD

MAY 2014

Work drinks.

The last thing I feel like. But Jason had insisted: "At least once a year, you need to let the team leave early to celebrate bedding down an issue. And you need to join them for at least one drink. Tonight's the night. No excuses."

I slide into the booth beside him with my glass of wine, and he smiles at me warmly. Grateful. Like I am in fact a human being, not a robot.

"How about a toast to this issue," he shouts out to the bar, and our crew cheer loudly in response. "Well done, everyone!" he continues, then he looks to me meaningfully. I roll my eyes at him and stand up.

"Thank you, everyone! For all your hard work and commitment once again! I know I flick the whip sometimes. But our product is the best. And that's thanks to you guys. So, well done!"

That is not strictly true. Our product is the best because I edit, design, primp, and preen it to within an inch of its life. These people? They might get the stories. But I make them sing.

I know it sounds arrogant. And it's not like I think I could do it without them. They are fabulous, and I know it. But everyone else in this room would be happy with "great." I'm the only one who insists on it being perfect.

Jason elbows me, a frown flashing across his face.

"I had to acknowledge I'm not the most encouraging boss." I shrug at him. "Otherwise suddenly shouting out thank you doesn't seem authentic. I know who I am. They know who I am. They're still here, because they get to do creative stuff, and this magazine is a feather in their cap. They should be thanking me for the opportunity," I grumble, mainly to annoy him.

"Your ego is beyond belief," he says, staring at me, rising to the bait.

I poke my tongue out at him and grin, and he shakes his head and laughs, his shoulders relaxing.

But I'm distracted by my phone ringing.

It's Kingston, and I throw it back in my purse, turning back to Jase.

"You're not going to answer that?" he asks.

"I spoke to him like an hour ago. He's getting kind of needy," I sigh.

Jase raises his eyebrows. "Really? I thought he was Mr. Perfect."

"Hmmm. I thought so too. But now he wants to talk to me or see me every five minutes. And I have a magazine to run. And frankly, I like having some time to myself. I feel like I can't even think at the moment, between work and him. A couple of times I've told him I need some quiet time, and he's turned up on my doorstep. With roses, like that makes it okay."

There's more, but I don't want to go into it with Jason.

The teariness, for a start. When I've asserted that I really meant it—I was exhausted, and needed some "me time"—he'd cried, said he felt unsure of my love, just needed to feel important to me.

Like his needs were more important than mine.

And I'd dithered—so unusual for me. I felt like I was watching myself. Somewhere, I knew this wasn't right. But I gave him the benefit of the doubt. That wickedly handsome, charming guy—maybe he wasn't as secure as I thought.

I felt a bit sorry for him.

I opened the door.

I let him in.

28

BEN

"Ben." Chloe looks surprised. It occurs to me that I don't think I've ever visited her before, except for family functions at her house.

That suddenly strikes me as a bit sad.

Only two years older than Ada and me, she just doesn't feature very prominently in my memories of family. Ada and Janey were both larger than life. In different ways, with vastly different degrees of appeal as newly acquired family members. But Chloe is hazy in my memories. Peripheral. Now that I think about it, I can't pin down a single distinct memory of her and me as teenagers, in the same house.

Odd, I think to myself, but Chloe is glancing behind her, looking slightly worried.

"Chloe, hi," I smile at her. "I wanted to have a chat. I won't keep you long."

"I'm a bit busy, actually, Ben. Do you mind coming back another time?"

That is actually really inconvenient. Chloe lives way out in the suburbs, in some ridiculous McMansion, with a cookie-cutter garden and something soulless shrouding the house. It's taken me forever to get here in peak-hour traffic on a Thursday night. I peer around her into a long, grey hall.

"Is Trevor here?" I ask, wondering what she's busy with, or if she just doesn't want to talk to me alone. It certainly feels awkward to me, so I imagine it does to her, too.

"No, he's out," she says softly, and I notice that her eyes are slightly puffy and red. She keeps them down, not meeting my eyes.

"Oh, Chloe, love. You're upset about something. Let me make you a cup of tea."

"No, really, it's okay. I'm okay."

"We don't have to talk about anything. If you don't want to. Come on. It's the least I can do. I'm excellent at cheering people up, it's my speciality." I smile at her encouragingly, at the exact same moment that I realise that you have to know someone well to be able to offer that service when things are rough. And I don't know Chloe well enough to make her laugh.

She stands aside, still looking at the floor, and I step inside and head to the kitchen. It's meticulously clean, much like Ada's. One thing the sisters have in common.

"White, with two, right?" I ask, pleased that I can remember at least this detail about her life.

"Actually, there should be some camomile. Weak, with a splash of cold water." Her voice is so soft. I stop, turn to her, worried, and she looks at me helplessly and starts to cry.

"Oh, shit, Chloe." Dumping the mug, I stride over to her, pull her into my arms, stroke her hair. She's a good head shorter than me, the perfect height to tuck under my chin and murmur soothing noises, kissing the top of her head.

We might not be close, but it kills me to see her cry. Largely because she must be feeling pretty fucking crummy to let me be the one to see it.

Huddled in my arms, she shakes silently, her distress probably doubled by trying to hide it from me.

"It's okay, love. You can cry as much as you want. Hey, you've seen me blub like a baby on enough occasions." I pull back and smile at her, holding her shoulders, and she smiles at least a little. Then I pull her back in and stroke her hair until her shaking subsides.

Finally she pulls away, her hair over her face. "How about that tea?" she says softly, not looking at me.

I busy myself at the sink, giving her a second to compose herself. Then I carry two mugs into her lounge.

"You want to talk about it?" I don't state the obvious. That I've never been the one she'd talk to about it. But hell, I'm here. And no one else seems to be.

Chloe lets out a long sigh.

"It's just the usual," she says.

"The usual? I'm not sure I know the usual."

She looks up at me then, surprised. "Ada doesn't tell you?"

I'm not sure what she's talking about. "Ada has told me you're pretty upset about these letters," I reply, carefully. "Is that it?"

Chloe looks out the window, chews on her lip. She looks nothing like Ada. Long, blonde, fine hair, usually pulled into a severe ponytail. Her features in general look more severe. She's beautiful, too, but in a different way. She seems harder, usually. Less soft, less fun.

She's shaking her head, carrying on some internal monologue that I'm not privy to, her lips moving slightly. I wonder if she knows she does this.

"Clo?"

"I'm surprised she didn't tell you," she says, something close to bitterness in her tone. "Maybe it's just not that newsworthy anymore."

I have no idea what she could be talking about, but before I can even start trawling through past conversations to try to work it out, she speaks again: "I had another miscarriage. It was the eighth."

I stare at Chloe in shock, my eyes pricking immediately. God. How awful.

"Oh my God, Chloe. I had no idea. I'm so sorry. That's heartbreaking." Suddenly her bright cheeriness, which always irked me, seems shattering. What she must have been covering up.

"We really thought this might be the one. I was fifteen weeks. The longest time ever. Everything was going well. All the tests were fine. It was a little girl—" On that she chokes, a sob escaping her, her whole body shuddering. But it's like some floodgate has opened. Even as she gasps and cries, she keeps talking.

I carefully take her tea from her and place it on the coffee table, sitting next to her this time, a hand gently rubbing small circles on her back.

"I've tried to stay positive. We're doing everything we're supposed to. We've given up caffeine, booze, fucking everything even remotely connected. Even black tea. Hence the camomile. Even Trev. Jesus, we haven't had a drink for nearly two years. And I get sick. So sick. It would be easier if we lost them earlier. But we almost always get to at least eleven weeks. And I go through the whole morning sickness. Except it's all-day sickness. And the exhaustion. And trying to work, and stay positive, and be friendly, and give a flying fuck what everyone else is doing. And we bought this fucking house with the big backyard for the fucking big family we were supposed to have. And I don't think I can do it anymore, Ben. *I. Am. So. Tired.* I am tired in my bones. I can't go to work tomorrow. Or Monday. Or maybe ever again. I just can't. And I can't face Mum, who hugs me and says sorry without an ounce of understanding, and pats me on the back and says *'you can try again,'* and *'at least you can get pregnant,'* like that fucking helps. Eight pregnancies, and I bet she says it again this time. I fucking bet you. And Trev, we've always held each other up, you know, we've always been the thing that saves each other, but you know I told him I don't think I can keep going, and he just can't bear it, he wants kids so badly. And I don't know how we can go on. It's like a full-time job, the worst one, the most horrible, shit-kicker job I can imagine. Trying to get pregnant. Being healthy. The sickness. The miscarriages. The appointments. Smiling at people, because they don't want to hear this horror. And even if they care, they can't understand it. How consuming it is. How this is our *whole lives*. It is *exhausting*. It's *shattering*. And I think I'm done. I'm forty this year. I. Just. Can't. Do. It. Anymore."

The pain radiating off her is killing me; I can almost feel it, hot and heavy and claustrophobic. And I'm telling myself I need to listen and be there for her, but I can't help it—a sob escapes me too. I pull her back into my arms and cry into her hair.

"I'm so sorry, Chloe. I'm so, so sorry," I sniffle. "God. And I'm sorry I'm crying. But I'm so sad for you." I clutch her tightly, like I can hug the hurt out of her. I can't believe I didn't know she was struggling with this.

Eventually, she pushes me off, smiling a little bit. "You always were a bit of a sook," she says. Then, clutching my hand. "Thank you. It actually is really nice you can cry with me. It's more than bloody Mum can do." She reaches for her tea, grimaces at it, then takes both mugs back to the kitchen and turns the kettle back on.

"It's just hard, letting go of your dreams," she says from the kitchen. "I just assumed I'd get married, have some kids, let work take a bit of a back seat for a few years. It never even occurred to me that that might not happen."

She brings back our fresh tea, sits back down next to me.

"I'm really surprised Ada never told you," she says, watching me.

"I think she'd consider that your story to tell," I say slowly. "It's a pretty personal thing for someone to share." I pause for a moment, then add: "I'm glad you told me."

"Me too." She smiles. "I guess I've always thought it was you and Ada, and I was the third wheel."

"I've always thought you disapproved, and didn't want anything to do with me," I counter.

This is more talking than Chloe and I have done in twenty-something years.

"I didn't really disapprove," she sighs. "I guess I was jealous. Not like that!" She blushes. "Just jealous that you guys were so close. It made sense, of course. You were the same age, in the same classes. But Mum was never around. You guys were always giggling in Ada's bedroom. I felt like I didn't have anyone. I guess it felt easier to be all snooty about it than to admit I was lonely." She stares off out the window, her face a little sad.

"I didn't know that," I tell her, surprised. "That you felt left out. I think it always felt like you were older and cooler and doing your own thing. And then you went off to university and seemed to have your own life. I guess I never really thought that before I came along, there was just the two of you. That you might have missed that."

We're both silent for a while, thinking. Then I ask what I came to ask—it's probably as open and honest as we've ever been with each other. It'll either keep this new intimacy going or send us right back to where we started.

Worth a shot, I figure.

"Why did you never tell Janey about Ada and me? Sometimes it felt like you and Ada were competing," I say carefully, not wanting to place responsibility for that anywhere. Hell, if I've learnt anything in the last hour, it's that things might not be how they seem. "If Janey is going to flip out as much as Ada thinks she is, it would have shot you way ahead in the good-daughter race."

Chloe stares at me for a while, her face a mask.

"How do you know I didn't?" she says eventually, a strange glitter in her eyes.

29

ADA

November 24, 2017

"Did he ever try to strangle you?"

"*Jesus.* Chloe. What the fuck?"

"It says here that your risk of death by intimate partner violence is far higher if there is a history of attempted strangulation. It's like a major red flag." She frowns. "That seems kind of obvious though, doesn't it? If someone tries to kill you, you ought to be worried?" She muses on this for a while, her expression more like she's pondering how it could be that someone doesn't like coriander than how being strangled isn't a red flag.

At least that means she's being thoughtful, rather than impulsive.

"You've dug out your research again, I see."

Chloe ignores me and continues.

"It also says that the period immediately after leaving the relationship is the most dangerous time for women. The time they will most likely be killed. So at least that danger period has passed. But I suppose this is all patterns. Generalisations. I'm sure there are outliers. It doesn't necessarily mean that you're safe. That *we're* safe," she adds, looking at me meaningfully.

"What are the stats on family members being killed?" I ask her, raising an eyebrow.

She frowns. "It's not a joke, Ada."

"I know." I sigh.

I nearly say something. Nearly tell her that I don't think Kingston is writing these notes. I've gone over and over it and I'm almost certain that it's not him.

So I nearly confide in her, ask for her help. But I'm not sure that I trust her.

Then again—surely she wouldn't waste so much time on her bloody family violence research if she knew Kingston wasn't writing these letters?

If, say, she knew who was?

But I don't say anything.

I don't know who to trust.

And I especially don't know if I can trust myself.

30

ADA – 34 YEARS OLD

July 2014

"It's been five months."

Ben is looking at me sadly. My heart lurches at hurting him.

But it's for the best, I tell myself.

"I thought we both needed some space from each other. To move on. It's hard to move on when we keep seeing each other."

"I don't want to move on."

"Ben. Fuck. I care about you. But I'm with someone else."

"You don't *care* about me. You love me. And you're trying to love someone else who your mother might approve of to...oh, who the fuck knows why."

This was not what I expected. It's unnerving, and makes me snappish.

It makes me feel sick.

I want, suddenly, to get away as quickly as I can.

"Fuck. I thought it would be nice to see you. I've missed you. But I don't need to listen to this. And fine. Yes, I don't want a partner that my family will disown me over. Okay? Maybe it shouldn't matter, but it does. You and I? We are not okay together. My family might not be great, but they're my family and I want to keep my relationship with them. That means giving you up. That's my choice. So it's up to you now. You call me if you think you can do the friends thing."

I push my chair out as I stand up, and it skids away from me and topples over.

"Ada, wait—"

But I'm already storming out of there, not even bothering to right the chair.

Furious with Ben because it's easier than being furious with myself.

WAITING FOR A TRAM, tapping my finger impatiently against my bag strap, I hear my phone pinging and have a strange flash of dread.

Interesting, I think to myself. *You think your boyfriend's texting you and you feel...dread?*

I'm still not entirely sure what I think about the whole situation. Is he just insecure and needs to be sure of my love before he can truly respect my needs? Or does he not really care about my needs?

Kingston: *Why can't I come and hang out with you and Ben? I haven't even met your brother.*

Dread is replaced with anger, and I shove my phone back into my purse furiously. Jesus, I can't have five minutes to myself without him wanting my attention back on him.

Is this normal though—what new relationships are like—while you work out the lay of the land? I've only ever been with Ben. And you can't really call that a relationship. It was a hidden thing. Beautiful and tender and hot as all fuck. But we didn't "date." There was no courtship, no getting to know each other. We snuck around having crazy hot sex. And we already knew each other inside out by the time we first hooked up.

Ping!

I snatch my phone back out of my bag in a rage. *What the fuck does he want now?*

Kingston: *I think it's unkind of you to leave me lonely tonight while you're out having fun. Let me just come by for half an hour. I need to see you.*

Yeah. No. This is not normal.

This is making me furious.

Then again, everything is making me furious tonight.

Me: *Kingston. I can't see you every night. I like my independence. I need time without you. We're having dinner tomorrow. I'll see you then.*

IT WENT DOWNHILL QUICKLY after that.

There was the time he knocked on my door at 2 a.m. He just woke up and was thinking about me and "thought it would be nice to cuddle," he said.

Then there was the time I told him I was having dinner with friends, and he wanted to know exactly who, and said he was "uncomfortable" with me going out with other men.

Do men really try to pull that shit? I'd thought to myself, astounded.

He texted in the middle of our dinner.

Kingston: *My doctor thinks I could be suicidal. That I shouldn't be left alone.*

What the actual fuck was that?

The threat was left there, hanging.

I didn't reply.

Within a week, I'd broken up with him.

We had only been together for five damn months.

It felt like a fucking lifetime.

Once I'd ended it, a litany of other things resurfaced. Things

I'd allowed, or made excuses for. His insisting on coming with me to social events where "men might hit on me." Perhaps it wasn't so glaringly obvious because I was always working, never socialising. Perhaps I might have clued on earlier if... I stop myself though. My therapist said that I can't blame myself for someone else's actions. That he was deliberately manipulating me, whether he was conscious of it or not.

That he was probably well practiced at it.

That I am not to blame for responding with empathy. For giving people the benefit of the doubt.

Hell, it's not a bad thing to believe that people are trustworthy.

He's insecure; I have to show my love more.

He really loves me and isn't used to feeling jealous; I have to help him learn to manage this. He's getting some counselling to help him. He's really trying!!

He's just a possessive person; do I really care if he doesn't want me to hang out with other men without him? It's not much to give up; I barely go out anyway.

"Women are often trained to make other people feel better, to put other people's needs first," she'd said. "It's part and parcel of mothering. It's expected. It's a cultural norm."

"I don't," I'd told her. "I put my magazine first."

She'd cocked her head at me, waiting. Because: why? Why did I put my magazine first? But that was a different conversation.

Nevertheless, I couldn't help but focus on my part in this.

Where was my good judgement? How did I miss all these signs? Worse, how did I see them and not act on them?

"You did act on them," my therapist had said.

But it wasn't because I was strong. Or more insightful than anyone else. Or less inclined to be a victim. My get-out-of-gaol-free card, really, was just selfishness.

I wanted fewer demands from a partner.

I wanted more time to myself. More time to excel. His needs

were starting to impinge on my ability to do the things that I valued.

Breaking up with him was easy.

What came after was the hard part. Getting rid of the guy.

And forgiving myself for my mistake?

That part... I still haven't managed that part yet.

31

ADA – 34 YEARS OLD

"Why are you still talking to him?" Chloe wants to know.

I ponder this.

"I do feel bad. He's so hurt. I feel guilty I suppose."

"But you can't be the person that supports him. Not when he wants the relationship and you don't. He can't move on if he keeps seeing you."

"I'm not seeing him. I said he could call me. Honestly, I just said it to get away from him. He was so clingy. I thought I had to offer him something to get him out the door. I didn't think he'd call six times a day."

There's more, but I don't want to tell Chloe about it. I feel stupid enough as it is. I don't want to highlight further how I—the queen of success—ended up with someone so...*icky.*

Icky is the only word I can think of. So needy and clingy and....*icky.*

Also, it seems to be a better word than scary.

Ending it had been easy for me, emotionally speaking.

But he had cried, and carried on. Said I owed him our relationship. That I'd made promises to him. Said that we'd talked about marriage and kids, as though discussing what we each wanted in the future was a promise to fulfil.

He said he had no one to support him through the break up, that I owed him at least friendship to help him through.

Said all sorts of crazy shit.

"I've stopped answering the phone. Hopefully he'll get the message and just go away. So I'm not talking to him anymore. We're in agreement. It's done, over. Let's talk about something else, okay?"

AFTER I STOPPED ANSWERING his calls, the text messages increased by about six hundred percent.

Kingston: *I'm so depressed. Please call me.*

Kingston: *If I kill myself it will be your fault.*

"An absence of physical violence does not necessarily mean a lower risk of harm for the victim," Chloe reads to me, curled up in the armchair in my office. I had eventually showed her the texts, told her about his turning up everywhere before I broke it off with him.

She's found all the reports. The latest research.

Kingston: *You never cared about me, you were just using me for money.*

That one was rich—because another warning sign I completely missed—after the first couple of months, he always managed to *forget* his wallet. "I'll pay you back," he'd say, mortified.

He never did.

"Probably an attempt to limit your finances, have you become dependent on him," Chloe said, reading more from her booklet.

"I think he was probably aware that a few dinners wouldn't drain my bank account," I had replied, rolling my eyes. I had thought her persistence with the booklet was over the top.

Me: *I'm sorry. It's over. Please stop contacting me. It might be helpful to talk to your doctor about how you're feeling instead.*

Replying was a mistake. It was like it was a green light in his mind. A ratio of texts-to-replies. That if he just sent another three hundred messages, then he'd be rewarded with another reply.

Kingston: *You're being so selfish. I don't need to talk to a doctor! I need to talk it through with you. You're the one who hurt me, so you should help me to feel better.*

Kingston: *You don't even have a heart. Anyone with a heart would help someone they've hurt through the pain.*

"You should never make contact!" Chloe yells at me, agitated. "You can't rationalise with an abuser!"

"Noted," I told her.

I didn't roll my eyes.

Kingston: *You said you wanted to have kids with me! You can't just say things like that and then change your mind.*

I changed my number.

He started calling the office.

Embarrassed, I told my PA to say, "Ada doesn't wish to speak to you," and terminate the call.

He pretended to be other people, but Casey learnt his voice soon enough.

Eventually, he turned to letters.

Long, rambling, incoherent letters. That didn't actually say much more than the text messages had. Just a longer version of all the things that he felt were my responsibility.

And when I still stayed silent, they became more threatening.

You'll come to a bad end.

"Does he mean he will orchestrate a bad end for me, or that, because I'm so unkind, it is inevitable that I will end up in a bad place?" I muse to Chloe over the phone the next week, with more bravado than I feel.

"Well, you shouldn't bloody wait around to find out. Get a restraining order. Talk to the police. In fact, I'm coming over. Let's just go down to your local station now and talk to someone."

"Chloe, I'm working—" But I'm talking to the dial tone. I sigh heavily. I know she's right. A vague sense of unease is permeating everything. But I have better things to do. I resent how much time this is taking up. I resent my own stupidity for dating such a nutjob in the first place. And I feel terribly, horribly guilty for inadvertently involving Chloe and Mum.

Nevertheless, unease prevails.

People think that until someone hits you, you're not in any actual danger. Control, manipulation—they're not taken seriously, I'm starting to learn.

But if you look at the research, many people killed by their lover hadn't experienced physical violence before the fatal attack. They'd experienced terror. Self-doubt. Coercion. Gaslighting. But the first physical attack was the deadly one.

The opposite is also true, of course. Many others are subjected to horrible physical abuse that culminates in death.

I've had a hard time with my therapist naming my first public relationship experience as family violence.

"Psychological abuse is still not recognised as family violence by the vast majority of people," she'd said.

That I believe; I don't even recognise it myself.

"He was just a jerk," I tried to tell her.

"What if Trevor treated your sister that way?" she'd asked.

That stopped me short. Gave me food for thought.

WE WAIT FOREVER at the station.

Finally, a bored-looking officer with receding hair and a notebook and pen usher us into a small, windowless room.

"So, tell me from the start," he says, not looking up from his notepad.

He takes notes as I fill him in. Interrupts occasionally with phrases that make me feel stupid and small.

"And when did he first hit you?"

"What? He didn't. He hasn't. His letters have become more threatening. I'm worried that the more I don't respond, the more he escalates."

"Right. So what happened next?"

Later, a perplexed look on his face: "So...that's it?"

Chloe bristles beside me, and I touch her arm.

"Look, it's been weeks since we broke up. He was texting fifty, sixty times a day until I changed my number. But he knows where I live and where I work. One of the letters asked if I had a nice dinner with my sister last week—like he was watching me. I'm scared, okay? That he'll be one of those guys who thinks, 'if I can't have her, nobody can,' and kills me. I know it probably seems small compared to what you're used to seeing. But..." My voice trails off. I suddenly feel like crying. I'm not used to not having people take me seriously. I'm not used to not being the one in control. But what do you do if someone just doesn't see reason? Simply does not allow you to make a decision? A decision as big as ending a relationship?

The police officer looks bored and disinterested. He puts his pad away.

"Look, there's not really enough for us to do anything at this point. He's not directly threatening to hurt you. There's no evidence he's done anything illegal. I think the best thing to do is keep in touch with us if it escalates further—if there's concrete threats, if he tries to get into your house or something."

"Well that's just great!" Chloe snaps, seething. "So we wait until he hurts her, then you'll do something? That's just fucking useless!"

"I'm sorry. We can't act unless there's been a crime committed or threats made. You can try applying for a restraining order, but I can tell you that I'm pretty sure that based on what you've told me, they won't grant one. And of course if you feel threatened, call the police."

"And what about those notes," I ask, indicating his notebook. "They get put in the system?"

He shakes his head slowly, watching me curiously.

"So if I call the police because he's at my house threatening me, whoever comes won't have any background, won't have access to any of that?"

"We can't record it against a person if we're not charging them with something." He shrugs, opening the door.

Chloe is staring at him, mouth agape, but I take her elbow and steer her out the door.

I feel choked up, but mostly on my own stupidity.

How did I let this person into our lives?

32

ADA

"I have a confession to make."

My head snaps up. My office, which is usually my haven, is like a merry-go-round this week. Family members popping up all over the place. What was that game that was around when I was a kid? Hitting some small rodent on the head every time one popped out of a hole.

That's what I feel like doing.

Cracking these bloody family members over the head every time they pop up, abrupt and unexpected. Chloe only left an hour ago, and she's back already, for God's sake.

I immediately think of the letters. Oh God, is she going to confess she's sending them, to, to...?

I'm not sure I'm ready for Chloe's confession. So I hurriedly jump in before she can say another word. It's a question that I've been pondering a lot this week, anyway.

"Why do you think Mum's so disinterested in us?"

It's Chloe's turn for the head snap. She stares at me, mouth agape.

"You haven't noticed?"

"I've noticed that she's disinterested in *me*. But no, I have *not* noticed that she's disinterested in *you*."

Now it's my turn to stare.

"What do you *mean*?" I ask her, bewildered. "Mum is like the least interested, least invested mother I've ever met. She's completely self-absorbed. She doesn't remember the first thing about my life."

"She's like that to *me*," Chloe counters. "But you—*God*. She *raves* about you. 'Ada did this, Ada did that, oh, my, isn't Ada so clever,'" she says in a falsetto voice, presumably imitating our mother.

I stare at her in disbelief.

"Mum has absolutely no idea or no interest in anything I do. She still doesn't even know what my magazine is about. She asked me to write a bloody tribute to Bill in it next month."

"Well, at least she knows you run a magazine, and can tell all her pals how clever you are," Chloe says, bitterness lacing her words. "She doesn't even know what I do. Doesn't matter that I'm the youngest national manager in the company *ever*. She never boasts about anything that *I* do."

I stare at Chloe some more. Aside from being patently untrue —I hear Mum throwing about both of our achievements as though they were her own, as though she was critical to their occurrence—her bitterness about it is shocking to me.

"Mum is always boasting about you," I tell her, incredulity all over my face. "With about equal genuine care or interest as she shows for me. Just enough to impress her friends. Not enough to make us feel like she actually sees who we are or cares about us. Actually being engaged with her kids has never been her strong point. Don't you remember as kids, she used to take off with her latest boyfriend for days at a time and not even say goodbye?"

Chloe is staring back at me, an odd expression on her face.

"I don't remember that," she says. "I remember she was always so excited to hear about your school work and your results. Even when I topped the class, she was excited for all of five seconds, then went straight back to find out how you were doing."

"No. You're remembering it wrong. That was *me*. The five seconds. It was the only time I ever had her attention. I tried so hard to top everything to get that skerrick of attention she'd shower me with for...yes...*five fucking seconds*."

Chloe is shaking her head. "No, *you're* remembering it wrong. She adored you. You couldn't do anything wrong. She helped you with your homework. She'd always just wave me away, tell me to ask the teacher for some extra help during lunch time. I was basically invisible."

"She *never* helped me with my homework," I say, completely gobsmacked that our versions of these events are so disparate. "The only time she ever came in when I was studying was to tell me something completely irrelevant. It felt almost like she was trying to distract me, rather than help me."

We stare at each other silently for a while.

"We were both invisible," I say eventually.

Chloe is looking at me strangely.

I'm probably looking at her strangely, too.

So Chloe thinks Mum cared more for me than her. Isn't that the middle child syndrome? Shouldn't that be my complaint? Or am I getting that wrong?

We both remain silent.

"What's your confession?" I ask eventually, not really wanting to hear the answer. But now I want to get away from *this* conversation. I need some more time to process the disconnect between our memories of our mother. Hold it up against our relationship, try to sort out what it means. If it means anything.

Chloe sits abruptly onto the floor, resting her back against a bookshelf. She closes her eyes for a second.

"The elephant," she says, not opening her eyes.

I'm confused.

"Your confession is that you know about Ben and me?"

No, that can't be right; I know she knows about that. And the last letter would have informed her if somehow she had missed it.

"No. But it's about that."

She pauses for a long time. Finally, she looks straight at me, that bold I-dare-you face I know so well. It's the face she uses when she wants to stand by her decisions, but she knows the recipient of the news is going to be pissed.

"Okay," I say, slowly.

"I guess it's a neat segue from the question you just asked me. I think maybe we have really different ideas and memories about Mum."

She pauses again, and starts doing that thing where her lips are moving, like she's carrying on the conversation without me. Or maybe she's rehearsing, I don't know. Either way, I'm left hanging.

"Clo?"

She sighs and looks back at me. "I told Mum about it."

"About what?"

She looks exasperated. "The elephant we never talk about. About you and Ben. Being together."

33

BEN

"Ada. Call me. I have some news."

After my conversation with Chloe, I'm dying to get a hold of Ada, but she's being incredibly elusive.

At the office, I delegate with wild abandon. I'm a big fan of delegating anyway, but today calls for even more flamboyance. I'm throwing tasks around like confetti at a ball.

"Zoe, you want to manage the final checks this issue? You could get a sense of all that responsibility!" I wiggle my eyebrows at her, mock-flirty, but she can see the plea beneath the movement.

"And?" she says, laughing, knowing there's something in it for me.

"And you'd be doing me a huge favour. I have something personal I need to take care of today. And the proofs really need to be approved by 5 p.m. at the very latest."

"Skiving off again?" She shakes her head, now her turn to be mock-disapproving. "That's been happening a bit lately, boss. Where's your commitment? And what about leading by example?"

I grin at her. She's been on my team for ten years. I trust her completely.

"I am. I'm giving my subordinates a chance to take the helm. It's important to show trust in your staff, and give them opportunities to stretch themselves, to progress. I actually don't have anything I need to take care of. This is in fact really just an excuse to give you that chance."

She laughs again, throws a pen at me. "Go on, get out of here," she says.

The spreads are covering my desk in huge glossy prints. They need to be checked for colour, pages, order, margins, run-on words, correct photos with the articles, etcetera. It's a long and tedious job. I lose interest in it quickly...hence the odd mistake sneaking through.

"I owe you big time," I call over my shoulder as I dash out the door.

"I want your job in a few years!" she calls after me, and I grin to myself. I really do love my team.

OVER AT ADA'S OFFICE, her PA shrugs apologetically.

"She said absolutely no interruptions."

I feel sorry for the girl. You really wouldn't want to disobey Ada. But I'm bloody going to talk to her. This cannot wait.

I wink at her, already up a few points by remembering her name. Probably more than Ada does. I laugh to myself, then walk to the door.

Which is locked.

I'm surprised. Apart from our kinky dalliances in there, I've never known Ada to lock her door. No one would dare interrupt her, except for me and Jason.

Maybe she really is worried about Kingston.

When my knock goes unanswered, I take out my phone and

call her for the tenth time. It goes straight to messagebank. I try her landline, but just get voicemail.

"Ada, Jesus, what are you doing in there? I'm going to start to get worried soon. Call me. I'm standing outside your office, and I'm not leaving 'til we talk. I've got something important to tell you."

Casey hurriedly glances away when I turn back around, pretending to be hard at work on something. When she sneaks another glance at me, I grin broadly. "Mind if I sit here? I'm going to wait her out."

She shakes her head nervously, looking back at her computer. I watch her, waiting. Eventually she peeks up at me again and looks embarrassed that I'm staring straight at her, catching her looking.

Sometimes I wonder about all those opportunities—all these women falling over themselves for me. I've never paid the slightest bit of attention. Ada has always been everything I've ever needed. It has been fun, sure. A chance to tease and flirt, always careful to mention that I'm not available somewhere. Throwing in "my girlfriend" here or there.

I grin again. "Do you know what she's doing in there? Why all the secrecy? Even on deadline she'll usually see me...if we have a conflict to work out," I hurriedly add, suddenly aware this isn't how I usually appear at Ada's office.

Casey shakes her head, looking too nervous to squeak, let alone risk Ada's wrath by talking to the enemy, no doubt.

If only she knew I was Ada's best, best friend.

If only everyone knew.

But maybe, maybe—soon they will.

34

ADA

November 24, 2017

I sit up sharply, my back ramrod straight in my chair, letting this sink in.

"You showed her the letter?" I say, faintly. Thoughts are crowding my brain, falling over each other, kneeing each other in the groin in their desperation to find some way out, find something to take comfort in. And avoid the horror that I feel rising up my throat.

I lurch for my waste-paper basket and dry retch into it, my brain just too terrified to compute this information.

"No," says Chloe, ignoring my gagging. "I told her a couple of years ago. It was just after our sixth miscarriage. I was crying. She was her usual unsupportive self. *'There'll be other babies!'* Then she just changed the topic to tell me about some wonderful thing you had done. I can't even remember what. And you'd just—"

"Wait, wait!" I cut her off, my shoulders heaving, the effort of breathing leaving me nothing left for speech. Taking a couple of panting gulps, I steady my hand on the desk and try again, my voice louder. "Two *years* ago?"

My scattered, terrified thoughts are starting to form sentences. Outraged, angry sentences.

"You didn't tell me this for *two years*? You betrayed my trust *two years ago*? You've carried on and refused to talk about it—"

"Let me—"

"No! I will not let you anything! I can't believe you! Why the fuck would you do that? Why—" My phone starts ringing, and I reject the call angrily, whirling back on my sister, but it starts ringing again. Ben. I switch it off, thinking he can wait. The desire to scream and shout and punch someone, bottled up for God knows how long, God knows about what, is crashing out of me. I'm ready to hurl shrapnel at this woman who, who—

"You'd just bloody let that lunatic into our lives!" Chloe shouts, before I can get my next word-blade out to cut her with. "And I'd just lost my baby! And all Mum could do was tell me how fucking wonderful you were! *Fucking. Perfect. Ada.* And—"

My landline starts ringing, and I pick it up and hurl it against the wall, the fury consuming me. I want to break things, hear them smash and scatter, feel the vibrations through the floorboards as they're destroyed.

Later, I would be able to think that she hadn't betrayed a trust, because I'd never extended it to her.

But in the moment I just wanted to make noise.

I turn on her, ferocious, furious: "And you just thought you'd—"

"Shut up, shut up, SHUT UP!" she shouts, leaping to her feet and sweeping all the papers and stationary and flotsam from my desk onto the floor with one expansive shove. My monitor wobbles on the edge for a moment, then crashes to floor, spidery lines shooting out from the corner across the whole screen.

I'm momentarily shocked into silence.

Into which I hear Ben's voice, ugly and raw, shouting through the door.

"Fuck you, Ada! FUCKING FUCK YOU."

35

ADA – 34 YEARS OLD

September 2014

"Your sister should pay for her interference."

That's the line that stands out.

Aside from that, there's more of the usual.

"We talked about marriage! You can't just commit to forever with someone and then walk away like they're a piece of dirt! You'd treat a dog better than you treated me."

And on, and on, and on.

Exactly how he thinks Chloe interfered isn't clear, but by now, I know there's no point bothering him with such pesky things as reality. What actually happened doesn't matter. What matters is what Kingston *believes* happened. Or what he believes should have happened next.

My reality—that's inconsequential.

All the things I had thought about myself until that moment are held up for me to see just how easily they can be erased. It's so bizarre it's almost funny.

What I want—irrelevant. Apparently, what Kingston wants matters more.

What I choose—irrelevant. I don't get a choice. Only Kingston gets that privilege.

My perceptions of myself and the world around me—completely, utterly, astoundingly irrelevant.

How Kingston sees it is the only thing that matters.

I'm a 34-year-old woman, the CEO of my own business, which I started from scratch. I'm wealthy, by anyone's standards. I look after myself. I run my whole life without any help from fucking anyone. And somehow, it feels like Kingston is erasing me. I can't even make sense of it. It is so ludicrous as to be comical, except it's not. Because he believes it. He believes it is his right to get what he wants, regardless of what I want. The arrogance, the entitlement is infuriating; the complete disconnect from reality is terrifying.

To him, discussing that yes, I wanted to get married one day was just as much a commitment as the actual ceremony itself.

I had heard about this stuff, of course. But it had never touched my life. Had never occurred in my circles.

Because I'm the only one stupid enough to choose a stalker for a boyfriend, I think to myself, cringing. I cringe every single time that word crops up.

Stalker.

I have a *stalker.*

I'm not the type of person who hooks up with a *stalker.* I'm successful. I'm organised. I don't take any shit from anyone.

How the fuck did I end up with a *stalker?*

And how did I not notice this person was *fucking insane???*

The thought goes round and round my head. It's inconceivable to me. I never make mistakes. And this is a big one. Not one I can sweep under the carpet. It's spewing out all over my life, my family. My work.

This mistake? It's shouting itself from the rooftops for everyone to see. It's a fucking New Year's Eve fireworks display and you can see it even if you're miles from the fucking action.

Ben keeps calling, and I long to fall into his arms more than anything in the entire world. He's the one person who I might talk to about this and not feel stupid. He'd hold me and soothe me and make me feel okay. But I can't drag him into this either. The police might think it's trivial, but reading this craziness...who knows what Kingston's capable of. His mind goes to such peculiar places that I can't trust social norms and reason to prevail.

Is he just hoping I'll live a miserable life? Or is he capable of hurting me? And those I love?

To top it off, Chloe has started reading me horrible stories about all the women killed by their partners or ex-partners.

"Do you know, one woman is killed *every week* in Australia by a partner or ex-partner? Did you know the most dangerous time for the woman is after leaving the relationship? Do you know how many men kill their children as revenge on their ex-partner for leaving them? This one guy *threw his daughter off a bridge* after his partner broke up with him. In *Australia.* Can you believe that? Is this even real?"

She goes on and on, her research getting darker and deeper, her reading list taken over by nonfiction family violence horror stories. She's taken up this problem so enthusiastically that I can't help but wonder what the payoff is for her. It's uncharitable, given how she's trying to help me.

But it feels a little bit like she's gloating about my mistake.

"YOU'RE LUCKY," Chloe says a couple of months later, her face serious. "We're lucky. Stalkers don't always just fade out. They don't suddenly become sane and rational. Generally, they need help. And no one notices until they've killed someone."

Chloe hasn't had a letter or an email redirected to her for two months.

I make agreeable noises, not looking up from my laptop. She

stays silent, picking tiny pieces off her muffin, popping them distractedly into her mouth. I ask after Trevor, trying to steer the conversation back in another direction.

Because though we haven't had any crazy letters, that doesn't necessarily mean that I haven't seen the King.

36

BEN

She's replaced me.

I can't fucking believe it.

The muffled shouting, the breakage, the crashes. Was that *our* recording playing in there?

Before I can even think, I scream, "Fuck you, Ada! FUCKING FUCK YOU," through the door and stalk out of there.

I'm so full of rage I can't even think straight.

I can't believe she would do this to me. That was *our* game, *our* private joke.

And *three weeks*? She managed to replace me in *three weeks*?

As I burst onto the street, all I can think is that I'm a fucking idiot for wasting all these years on her. For believing in her. In us. For believing in love. Believing that she'd choose me, eventually.

Well. Fuck that. I can replace her just as easily.

And make her feel as crucified as I do.

37

ADA

For a second I'm gobsmacked.

Ben, swearing at me in public.

Not part of a game.

And then my brain catches up and I think, *shit.* He thinks I've got some other guy in here.

The anguish in his voice sends me scrambling to the door, to let him know it's just bloody Chloe. But when I open the door, fumbling with the lock, glancing back at Chloe who's collapsed in a wet, sobbing mess on the floor, he's already gone.

"Call him back for me, please, Casey," I say, rushing back into my office, other pressing questions crowding in on me.

"What did Mum say?" is the first one out of my mouth, trying to rein in my frustration. Chloe is in no state to talk. She's in the foetal position, snot running onto her lip, her breath coming in short little rasps, shoulders shaking.

"Everyone always lo...lov...loved you best," she stutters, her shaking increasing in intensity. "No matter what you did, you were always good, perfect, wonderful Ada. Getting good grades. Starting a magazine. So pretty you could have been on the cover of it. Boys falling all over you. And I'm not excusing it. I'm just trying to explain. That day. When I felt like I might die of sadness. I can't explain it to you. The anguish of losing a baby that I treasured. Everyone is so blasé about it. Like it wasn't a real baby yet. But it was real to *me*. It was my whole life. And it was the sixth time. And when Mum just changed the subject to how wonderful you were—when we had all these threatening letters from your fucking weirdo ex-boyfriend—I guess I just wanted her to not see you as perfect. Just for a moment. A day. I didn't want to hurt you. I didn't even think about it. It just came out. I think I just wanted to be equal with you for once. Like we were both human. Not you on a pedestal and me on the ground. Both of us, on the ground, where life happens and things are messy and nobody's perfect."

She looks so sad my anger evaporates, gone as quickly as it appeared.

"Clo—"

She waves me away, looking broken and small.

"She didn't even miss a beat," she says, her tone bitter. "That's all you want to know, right? If Mum still thinks you're perfect? The good daughter? Someone to brag about?"

My shoulders sag, and I slide down the back of the desk onto the floor beside Chloe and stare at the ceiling.

We don't touch.

We don't speak.

My mind moves sluggishly around this idea of mismatching memories. Or maybe how we perceived our own realities was the culprit, and our memories were never going to match up if we perceived things differently. Perhaps our realities were defined by how we viewed the world, and our memories likewise shaped by the way we saw things.

Strangely, this disconnect actually makes Chloe feel a little closer to me than she has in years.

"Well, I'm not that good," I tell her eventually, my voice flat. "Does that help? Because there are a few more mistakes I made that you don't know about when it comes to Kingston."

38

ADA – 34 YEARS OLD

OCTOBER 24, 2014

"God, you look good," says a low voice from the backseat.

I scream, my heart exploding in my ears, my hands scrabbling for the door handle, my body feeling like it's stuck in treacle, or one of those bad dreams where everything happens in slow motion. My mind is already rifling through my options.

Car park: deserted.

Inner city streets at 9:30 p.m. on a Monday: deserted.

Option to just run: need to ditch the heels.

But the feeling of a cold metal cylinder in between my shoulder blades stills me.

"I didn't want to pull this out," he says, conversational. "I only brought it in case you wouldn't talk to me."

My mind is still spinning at incredible speed.

If that is the case, would he shoot me if I ran?

Does he really want to kill me?

Is it better that he kills me here, where he can't hide me away, and at least he will get caught? My family will know what happened? Ben will—but that thought slows everything down, the roar inside my head deafening. My mind recognises that I shouldn't go there.

Instead, should I try to stay calm and try to find out what he wants?

But in the end, my body makes the decision for me. I throw up, lunging sideways so that my vomit lands across the passenger seat and the passenger floor, the rank stench of it hitting my nostrils almost immediately and making me retch further. I feel dizzy with fear. I have an overwhelming urge to close my eyes and rest a little. Sleep, even.

Gasping for breath, I try to steady my body and my thoughts. *Stay alert,* I berate myself. *Stay alert. You can outsmart this dickhead.*

Buying time, I stay hunched over the console, the handbrake poking into my tummy, my hair across my face, the reek of vomit burning my nostrils, the aftermath of it burning my throat.

Kingston rubs my back with his free hand and I flinch involuntarily.

"I've surprised you. I'm sorry. This isn't how I imagined our first conversation together to go."

I keep quiet. Given how clear I've made it that I don't want him in my life, how he imagined this conversation going is probably more terrifying than illuminating.

I cough and spit.

"There's a towel in the boot...?" I whisper, my voice hoarse, my throat scratchy. I'm still gulping in air, trying to look even more shaken than I feel. Which is pretty shaky.

"Here," he says, handing me some travel tissues he pulls from his jacket pocket. Like they'll do shit all to manage this mess.

"I need to clean the car," I say weakly, my mind already skipping to new horrors: this smell reminding me of this moment for the rest of my life.

As long as that life is, I think to myself, and shudder.

"What do you want, Kingston?" I'm still gasping for oxygen, that terror that comes with vomiting sometimes—that you can't get enough air in. That there's no time to breathe. On top of the panic and adrenaline, my body doesn't feel like mine at all.

"This is really uncool." I try to keep my voice level, normal, like we're just having a chat. Like it's just a bit weird and he'll realise and he could get out now and I'll drive off and we'll pretend everything is just fucking fine.

"I just want to chat. I don't think you understand a few things, and you never gave me a right of reply. You just shut off communication. So I want my right of reply. We're just going to go and have a chat. I've got a nice champagne on the yacht. Remember how we used to go out on the bay and drink champagne and eat fresh salmon?" He sighs with some remembered satisfaction. "I remember your hair in the sea wind. Red against the blue. Magnificent."

He sounds possessive, ardent.

He sounds fucking insane.

"It's late. Can we talk tomorrow? I don't want to go sailing in the dark. Just say we crash?"

"We won't crash." Kingston's tone is relaxed and strong. Sure of himself. There's no sign of the whiny, teary guy who'd begged for love or an audience those last few weeks we were together.

It's because he's in control and he knows it, I think to myself. *Fucking get yourself a gun if you want to feel all manly, huh.*

"I can't drive," I whimper, wondering how the role reversal will affect him. Him: the boss, me: distressed. With no power.

He rubs my back, the gesture somehow nauseatingly familiar and intimate. Possessive. I feel like I'm going to upchuck again and lean over, pulling slightly away from his touch, dry-retching into the seat beside me.

He notices the movement though, his voice taking on a steely edge, and I kick myself. I need him to let his guard down. Feel like he's winning. Not feel like he's being rejected. "Sure you can, princess," he says, pushing the muzzle of the gun into me again, a little harder this time. "Let's go."

I had thought about this, believe it or not. Forward-planning what I'd do. Anxiety experts would say that this is not helpful—ruminating on what-if scenarios.

But they hadn't met Kingston.

All that ruminating might just come in handy now. The options hang in my mind's eye, as clear as the day I concocted them.

Firstly, just get out and run. I didn't think he'd really kill me. That would defeat his purpose. His ludicrous, mindboggling, terrifying belief that we were meant to be together and all he had to do was convince me.

Secondly, ram the car into someone else at an intersection. If we couldn't drive, he'd have to run. Or would he shoot someone else, steal their car, and drag me into it?

Third, just jump out of the car. I'd rather die in the middle of the bloody road than endure whatever a deranged stalker has in store for me. Vague memories of Mum watching *The Bold and the Beautiful* had come to mind on more than one occasion in my ruminations. Cages, where the heroine remained until she "realised" that of course she loved her captor! She just needed him to remind her, that was all!

But in the moment, I do none of these things. And all I can put the choice down to is fear. Fear and hope, perhaps. Fear of hurting myself. I'd like to say I didn't want other people to get hurt, but I don't care about them right now. I don't want to crash and accidentally kill myself or do irreversible damage. I don't want to fall onto the bitumen, my skin splitting open, my face, my teeth unrecognisable.

Other people? They don't even rate a thought right now.

And hope? That maybe he just wants to talk. Maybe the safest thing to do is let him, while watching for my window.

So, trying not to wet myself, I start to drive.

ON THE BOAT, he lights a candle on the table. Fresh peonies spill out from a vase exuberantly. A bottle sits on ice on the white tablecloth, condensation running down the exterior, leaving a wet rim around its base.

Kingston looks at me nervously—*hopefully*—and it strikes me that he still thinks, with a little approval from me, that he can get our relationship back on track. Like forcing me here at gunpoint isn't a deal-breaker. Like this is just a date with a woman who's a little bit resistant, but "she'll come round."

But maybe that's my window. He really believes he can win me back. If I play along...maybe he'll relax his guard. Maybe I can escape.

Fuck knows how you escape a man with a gun if you're not in a movie. But I don't know what else to do.

So I smile at him, trying to convey anxiety but also that I'm touched by how much effort he has gone to. Like I'm open to his overture.

Like I'm all fucking ears to hear what he has to say.

39

ADA

"There's something I didn't tell you about Kingston."

Chloe leans up on one elbow, looks down at me. I can't read her expression.

"I've never told anyone this," I say, rolling to face her. "I'm not sure it's a good idea to tell you. At least now you can truly say you don't know."

But while I'm trying to work out where to start, Casey interrupts us, looking around the door. I'm shocked for a moment, thinking she's used the master key to open my door. But then I remember I dashed out there after Ben earlier. I must have forgotten to lock it again.

"I'm so sorry to disturb you, Ada," she says, her voice barely audible, her eyes darting all over the place. She looks terrified. "I knocked…?"

For the first time, I feel a pang of regret that I haven't made more of an effort to make my staff feel valued and safe.

"It's okay, Casey. But it's not a great time. Can it wait?" My voice is gentle, and Casey looks at me with a cross between hope and fear on her face. Hope that I'm genuinely being kind? And fear that it's the prelude to a tongue-lashing?

God, I really am an asshole.

"No," she squeaks. "Bill called. It's Ben. He's been hit by a car. He's being taken to the Royal Melbourne. Bill said he'll meet you there."

IN THE TAXI, Chloe holds on to my hand too tight, tears spilling down her cheeks in silent devastation.

"He'll be okay. He'll be okay," she repeats over and over, though whether she's trying to soothe herself or me is unclear.

"He came to see me," she says suddenly, clutching my hand even tighter. "We talked about the miscarriages. It was nice." She turns to face me. "You never told him?" But she doesn't wait for me to answer, turns back to stare out the windscreen. "He sobbed like a baby. It was...nice. I realised it was the first time we'd ever spent together as adults without anyone else in the family along."

She cries quietly for a while. I hold her hand absently, a terrible numbness settling in my chest. For a moment I have the strange sensation that she's having my feelings for me—that she's stolen them, even. That the whole family has, by not giving us their blessing. By being so hung up on appearances that we can't be together, Ben and I.

But Janey has known for two years? Why did she never say anything? Did she just not care? Did she maybe not hear Chloe? That wouldn't be a first. You miss things when you're not a good listener.

Chloe's grip, which has been slowly loosening on mine, suddenly squeezes my hand painfully tight again.

"Is that really the only reason you're not together? Thinking Mum will disapprove?"

I don't really know what to say. After decades of determined silence on this subject, Chloe's sudden interest is disorientating.

"I suppose so. I didn't want to be excommunicated."

I keep focused on that. The family. Disapproval. Shy away from the terror of where we're headed. How hurt Ben is.

Chloe turns to face me, adding her other hand to the tight, sweaty ball of touch that is supposed to be comfort for one of us, but exactly who remains unclear.

"You know how ridiculous that is, right? If what you say is true...about how Mum treats you...then we're basically excommunicated anyway. How much worse would having your stepbrother as your lover be?"

"Shhh," I hiss at her, nodding toward the driver, my cheeks growing hot, and a squirmy, uncomfortable tightness settles in my tummy.

Chloe continues to stare at me with something akin to understanding spreading across her face.

"It's not really Mum that's the problem, though, is it?"

I don't know what hidden gem she thinks she's latched onto, but I hurry to set her straight.

"Don't you remember that time with the Petersons?" I prompt her. They were old friends of Mum's. They lived in Perth and we rarely saw them, but Mum could often be found cackling on the phone to Dawn late at night during our childhoods, their mirth the only time I ever caught a glimpse of a younger, more carefree, more connected Mum. She had met Dawn at university (though Mum had dropped out shortly afterwards, after meeting a law student...my father) and their friendship had survived the wear and tear of time and distance.

Shortly after Mum had married Bill, Dawn's family had come for a visit, except for her husband, whose whereabouts she waved away like a pesky cobweb when Mum had asked about him.

"Working or something, who knows," she'd said elusively, and I heard nothing more about it.

The visit wasn't particularly memorable. Dawn's kids, about our age, were nonetheless not like us in any other respect. *Princesses,* Chloe labelled them dismissively to me later. *Morons,* I had corrected her, their lack of interest in school or achieving anything useful horrifying to me.

Nevertheless, Mum had insisted we spend a precious week of the school holidays together, showing them around the city and playing tedious games like Monopoly and Twister. I was crawling the walls by the last afternoon.

It was during the farewells that Mum made the comments that Chloe seems to have forgotten.

"We were all eating biscuits having some bloody grand farewell, Mum promising that we'd all go visit them the next holidays. You and I were rolling our eyes at each other, thinking we'd die if we had to spend another week with them and their precious fancy shoes and skirts. And Ben wandered past to his room, just wearing board shorts, and Dawn got this godawful look on her face watching him, kind of sly and leery, and said something to Mum and Mum killed herself laughing. I don't know what she said. But then Dawn said something about he'd be a nice husband for one of her girls. 'Gonna be a looker, that one,' she said, or something like that. And Mum was snickering to herself, but then she said—I've never forgotten—'As long as my girls don't get any ideas. There's nothing more disgusting than siblings getting it on.' Then they started talking about *Flowers In the Attic,* that book about siblings doing exactly that—and they were so outraged and disgusted. And Mum looked right at me and said 'He'll probably be the only boy that one ever talks to, given she never leaves the house. But stepsiblings are just as bad as siblings, isn't that right, Dawn?' And they both keeled over laughing some more."

Chloe has stopped crying and is looking at me with a shocked kind of expression on her face.

"I know, right? Mum was really freaked about the idea."

"That's not why I'm staring at you," Chloe replies. "I'm staring at you like you're an idiot because...you *are* an idiot."

She doesn't get a chance to explain, though, because we've pulled up at the hospital.

At least the conversation was a bit of a distraction from what is waiting for us here.

My heart lurches in my chest.

Suddenly, whatever Mum thinks or doesn't think seems irrelevant. Wasting time even remembering that conversation seems ridiculous. Ben is in hospital. Hurt. *And oh my God, just say he's really hurt? A pedestrian hit by a car—how well do they ever come out of that collision? What hope does a body have against a car?*

And mostly, mostly what I think is—*what's life worth if Ben isn't in it?*

To my surprise, Mum is in the waiting room with Bill.

His face is ashen, his eyes red and puffy. Bill has no trouble showing his emotional side. He grabs me in a big bear hug, but I get the sense that it's he who is seeking comfort, rather than giving it.

"Thanks for coming, girls," he says gruffly as he crushes Chloe in a similar hug. "There's not much news yet."

"What do you mean?" I ask, aghast. "You mean we can't see him now?"

"He's in surgery," Mum explains, rubbing Bill's back.

"Surgery?" I repeat, faintly. "What for?"

"Swelling in the brain. He took a nasty hit to the head. They need to relieve some pressure in his skull cavity, or something."

I feel the wind rush out of my lungs. I might as well have been hit by a car myself, the impact feels so sudden and so crushing. I stagger to the nearest chair, my voice barely a whisper.

"Was he okay? Talking? When they brought him in?"

Bill starts to sob quietly. Mum leads him back to a chair, sits with her arm around him.

"No, darling," she says gently. "He was unconscious. They suspect multiple fractures around his legs, maybe his pelvis. They've done x-rays and we're expecting to talk to the doctor after the surgery. We'll get more information then."

For once, Mum seems to be clear and attentive. Focussed on the important information rather than the petty fluff that she usually occupies herself with. I sit, my mind working overtime. Ben, lying in surgery. Bright, vivacious, larger than life Ben—with swelling on his beautiful brain.

Being operated on.

Believing I was with another man today.

But just as the panic and the terror starts to feel overwhelming, Chloe shrieks.

"Oh my God! Oh my God! Oh my God!" she says, pointing at me with wide, terrified eyes. "Was it Kingston, do you think?"

And suddenly all three pairs of eyes are looking at me questioningly. As though I might know.

As though I might be to blame, maybe.

Chloe snaps her head around to Mum, her eyes frantic. "What did they say? Was it a hit and run? Was it an accident or deliberate? Have the police spoken to you?"

Mum looks at Chloe thoughtfully while she digests this possibility, looking worriedly at Bill. But Bill is still watching me, a strange expression on his face. He looks like he's about to say something, but changes his mind and puts his head in his hands, instead.

"It doesn't matter right now, Clo," he mutters. "Let's concentrate on how Ben's doing first, okay?"

"Of course it matters!" Chloe cries. "We need to know whether we're in danger or not. Should I warn Trev? Can we go home safely? Do I need to call the police?"

Bill raises his head. He looks tired. He glances at me again.

"Have you had any more letters, love?" he asks me, an apologetic look on his face. He's handling Chloe remarkably well, all things considered.

I shake my head.

He looks back to Chloe, shrugging in an uncertain kind of way. "Maybe it's better to be safe and careful. The police want to see him when he wakes up. Let's talk to them then. But from what we were told, it sounds like he just stepped out in front of car."

Because he was upset about me, I think to myself, my heart lurching.

Chloe grabs her bag and trots into the adjoining hallway, and I can hear her muttering and wailing to Trev. But everything is going too fast for me. All I can think about—painfully, painstakingly—is Ben.

Ben and the whole host of uncomfortable, disorienting feelings that come with finally facing what really matters.

40

ADA – 34 YEARS OLD

OCTOBER 24, 2014

Kingston reaches across the table and takes my hand. He's hesitant, which seems ridiculous, given he has a handgun on his lap.

He strokes the back of my hand, slowly at first, but with increasing confidence and pressure.

"God, Ada, I've missed you," he whispers hoarsely.

My heart is pounding in my chest, the impulse to recoil from him consuming me. I don't know how long I can keep up the pretence of being open to the possibility of being together. But I can't see any other way to get the fuck away from him.

For someone who's never bothered to hide scorn, indifference, irritation, or anything in between, hiding what I really feel is going to be difficult.

"It's just a bit of a shock, that's all," I whisper, shivering with nerves. He notices, thinks it's the chilly air off the Bass Strait. He shrugs off his jacket and stands to place it around my shoulders, his hands lingering there. There's a message in that gesture. Longing—but also ownership.

I don't think Kingston is asking me a question. I think he's staking a claim on what he thinks is his.

I lean back into him for a moment, closing my eyes, gathering my resolve. Hoping that the gesture looks like I'm letting my guard down for a moment. I can feel him relax into me. I feel a kiss against my forehead. Then his cheek is pressed to mine.

"I wanted to take it slowly," he mutters. "I wanted us to start again. But I want you so badly, Ada. I *need* you. Now. Please. Come to my bed."

My eyes fly open and I jerk away from him—I can't stop myself.

He pulls back.

"I've shocked you," he says. But he grips my shoulders tightly. His need is palpable. "But remember how good we were together? How good in bed?" His voice drops, and I can feel his hard-on pressing into my back. He doesn't try to hide it. "Oh God," he groans. "You couldn't get enough of me, of my cock. Please, Ada. I know I've scared you. But don't make me wait."

And—unbelievably, unbearably—I wonder if this is the way to save myself.

It's ludicrous, if it is. That he wouldn't entertain the idea that I might fake it then run for it. Get the gun, though God, I've no idea how to use one. Could I fake that too? At least enough to get away?

Is it stupidity, I wonder to myself. *Or is this my only chance?*

STILL NOT SURE I can bring myself to do it—let alone do it convincingly—I try to buy some time. I can barely think through the roar of my own panic. The thought of kissing him—let alone fucking him—makes me feel like I'm going to vomit again. I lean back into him, closing my eyes, shaking my head slightly. Hoping it looks like confusion rather than trying to shake off the nausea on my face.

"Can we just talk a bit first? Hold hands a bit longer?" I ask softly, keeping my eyes closed, trying to breathe deeply. "It's just a bit unexpected. I'd like to hear your plans for us. If you're really serious." Slowly I open my eyes and turn to look up at him.

He groans again, grabs my hand, covers it in kisses. Sits back down opposite me without letting go of it and grins sappily into my eyes. "Of course, you gorgeous woman. You could ask me for anything. I'm yours. I always will be."

And just like that, I know I'm in with a chance.

He wants to hear this so badly.

So badly that he believes it is true.

WE SIP AT CHAMPAGNE, and I tell him about the magazine. I tell him I've been celibate since him. How I'd regretted my decision to put the magazine first. That I had thought I'd needed more "me time," but work seemed emptier with no one to share it with.

At one point he launches himself across the table, gripping the back of my neck and placing a chaste kiss on my lips, holding it hard against me for what felt like an hour, but must have only been seconds. His eyes closed, rapturous.

"I knew it!" he says, when he finally releases me. "I knew we were right together. I knew you must miss me. I knew I had to come back for you. I knew you'd see it eventually."

He's holding both my hands now, and I'm wondering where the gun has ended up. I didn't see it when he stood up to give me his jacket. I can't surreptitiously glance around for it either—Kingston's eyes are glued to mine with the joy of a dog, who thought he'd been left behind, discovering his owner was merely fussing at the door. They're adoring, full of love and lust and hope and satisfaction.

The satisfaction of someone who has finally been vindicated. Three months and a whole lot of crazy later.

"What about you?" I ask, trying to stare back at him with equal adoration. "Have you dated anyone?" I try to look worried, jealous, biting on my lip, looking down at my lap. Cause you'd ask that, right? If you were about to get back together? Check out the competition? If you were being normal?

Or are there no guidelines, when the ex in question is completely insane? Because you wouldn't be getting back together in the first place?

"Just a couple of girls," he says, his eyes not leaving mine. "They both wanted to marry me. One kept sneaking the condom off. I think she wanted to trap me. But I couldn't forget about you, my love." He grips my hand tighter, bouncing up and down in his seat with some kind of joy.

I lurch in my seat. Hopefully he thinks it's horror at the thought of him having sex with someone else. Rather than bile rising in my throat that he would think that's a normal thing to share with me.

He's completely fucking lost his mind.

Does he really think anyone buys this shit?

I grip his hands back, frown earnestly. "Two girls?" I mutter, wincing. "Are you sure? Are you sure about us? Really sure?"

And the moment I've been dreading. "Come here," he says, standing, pulling me gently to my feet. Then a whisper: "Let me show you." Then he's kissing me. Really kissing me, his tongue hungry in my mouth, his hands holding my waist like I'm the most precious, fragile gift he's ever been given.

But his mouth is famished. I give myself up to it, my hands tentatively finding his neck, pulling him into me. I can feel his cock against my crotch, and close my eyes, kissing him passionately, but feigning modesty around my nether regions.

I can do this, I chant to myself silently.

I can do this. I can do this. I can do this. To get away.

When he finally pulls away from me, his eyes are dancing with love. I think I can buy a bit more time, see if there's another chance. Another way. But the lead feeling in my stomach tells me otherwise.

I can't think of another way.

My thoughts feel cumbersome, heavy, like trying to crawl through thick fog with mud sucking at your feet, your legs.

"See?" he whispers, his hands moving slowly lower, finding my arse. "See what you do to me? There's never been anyone like you, before or after." He's trying to pull me against his cock, and I can't bear it. I swallow down a sob.

I must. I must. I must.

"Okay, I believe you," I take a deep breath, gather myself, then laugh, smiling up at him, resisting his grasp. "But before we go to bed"—here I smile at him shyly—"we need to talk about how you got me here. You really scared me. I don't want you to force me to do anything, ever, ever, ever again. You have to promise me?" I stare into his eyes earnestly, wondering if he's still buying this.

Strangely, I find it as equally terrifying as his gun-wielding, that I think he is.

Because if he's that insane, that disconnected from reality, then I just don't know what he's capable of.

He frowns. "I thought you might refuse to talk to me again. I tried for a long time, you know." His voice is suddenly petulant, whiny. I don't want him to think about that.

About how many opportunities he actually gave me to change my mind.

About how suddenly I've capitulated now.

Whether his gun might be the differentiating factor here.

My hands creep around to his butt, and I pull his cock into me firmly, staring up at him. I reach up on tiptoes, nibble at his jaw, and he groans, grabbing handfuls of my arse hungrily. "I'm sorry," I murmur, continuing to nibble along his jawline, then proceeding to run kisses down his neck. "You promise to get rid of the gun. I'll promise to never not talk to you, ever, ever again."

He's groaning, grinding his cock into me, his urgency increasing.

I could feign going for my champagne and make a run for it.

Or I could try to keep him drinking, fuck him, and wait until he sleeps.

Groaning myself, because I know I don't really have a choice, I find his lips, my kiss fierce, my tongue wrestling with his. His hands are everywhere—my breasts, my thighs, my head, my hair. He walks me forcefully back into the wall, pressing against me, kissing me frantically.

Pushing him off me, I reach for his belt, start to fumble with it, look up at him through my unruly hair.

"Do you promise?" I say, pretending to struggle with the belt. Pretending I just need to hear it before he can sink his cock into me, before we can get married, have babies, the whole nine yards.

He looks down at me, looks drugged, looks lost in lust and disbelief.

"Promise," he mutters, his voice guttural, barely contained.

"Throw it overboard for me. Please. Now. So I feel safe." I've got his zipper undone, am reaching around the back of his underpants, my hands finding his bare arse, my breathing deliberately heavy, panting into his chest, looking up at him, my mouth open, with what I hope looks like uncontained lust. But he frowns slightly, a flash of uncertainty passing across his face.

"Now?" he asks, the drunk look fading from his eyes.

I make the decision, don't even hesitate.

"After," I pant, my fingers finding his cock, groaning as I fist him, my head falling back in fake ecstasy to finally have that cock in my hand. After all this time. "I need you. Now. I can't wait," I add, just to be sure he's convinced.

He's upon me again, his groan lost in my mouth, his arms coming around my waist, hoisting me up, carrying me backwards to the bedroom, feasting on me the whole way. He throws me onto the bed, ripping his shirt off, falling on top of me. I struggle onto my elbows, fumbling with my shirt. He helps me, yanking it over my head, pausing for a second to feast his eyes on me, then he's hoisting my skirt up, pulling my panties off, running a finger along my cunt.

He moans as his mouth finds mine again, pressing a finger inside me.

"Fuck me," I moan, spreading my legs for him, arching my back, closing my eyes.

So I don't have to look at him.

So I can pretend I'm somewhere else.

He pushes his cock into me and fills me up.

41

ADA

Janey knows.

Is that why Bill is looking at me strangely? He thinks that Kingston might target my lover?

But why have neither of them ever said anything?

The afternoon has drifted into evening.

A doctor reported earlier that in order to relieve the pressure around Ben's brain, they drilled a small hole in his skull and inserted a tube to drain fluid.

They're now re-setting his fractures. One leg is broken in four places. The other, miraculously, is just badly bruised. His pelvis has also been spared.

They'll update us when he's out of surgery.

Chloe continues pacing.

We can't see him.

We just have to wait.

To my surprise, even Mum stays in the waiting room, stretched out on a row of plastic chairs, holding Bill's hand. He sits, staring vacantly at the wall.

Eventually, unable to bear the waiting and the pacing, I ask Chloe to take a walk with me.

"Call me if you hear anything," I tell Bill. I don't even look at Mum.

"I need to tell you something." I launch into it as soon as we're out the sliding doors. "I need you to stop pacing."

She looks at me blankly. "I'm going as soon as Ben's out of surgery. I need to be with Trev. You guys can talk to the police. We'll go stay with his parents or in a motel or something—"

"You don't need to," I cut her off. "That's what I'm trying to tell you."

"What do you mean?" She turns toward me, but doesn't stop walking, taking short, jerky little steps, jitteriness infusing her whole being. Instinctively, her middle finger goes to her mouth.

I haven't seen her chew on her nails for a long time.

"This isn't Kingston," I say, reaching out to take her hand, to halt her jerky steps and nail chewing. To force her to face me.

"How do you know?" She's not listening, her eyes darting around, already dismissing my statement as wishful thinking.

The pesky younger sister who never knows best.

Here is neither the place nor the time. I want to be with Ben. I want to sort out the thoughts and feelings that are bubbling up from somewhere hidden. The strange sensation that I've had it all wrong, all this time.

But I owe it to my family to relieve them of their fear, if I can.

So I jump straight in, hoping to tell this story as quickly as possible, with minimal fuss, and get back to Ben. Though in reality, I know that that's unlikely.

This story: it's going to cause a fuss.

"Because I saw him one last time after all the letters. And things didn't go the way that I had expected. But I can promise you—he wouldn't be sending any more letters."

42

ADA – 34 YEARS OLD

OCTOBER 24, 2014

Afterwards, Kingston fist pumps the air.

"That was as good as I remember," he gloats, shaking his head, squirming with joy, his cock limp across his thigh, his cum leaking out of me.

It feels like I've just run an emotional marathon. But I can't collapse yet.

I roll toward him, smiling lazily.

"You sure remember how I like it," I purr, pressing my tits against him. He groans into my neck, then pulls away.

"Let's set those beauties free," he says, staring hungrily at them, pulling the cups down to free them, massaging them roughly, his hunger already rising again. "God, I love your tits," he says.

I hope he's not thinking about a second round. My heart sinks when I remember the man's stamina.

Feigning playfulness, I straddle him, slowly reaching behind me to undo my bra. Then I shrug my tits back into my bra cups, laughing, flirting. "I'll get them out when you bring me a drink," I say, and he jumps up, his cock slapping his thighs as he hurries butt naked out onto the deck. He comes back a moment later with the bucket of champagne. "There's another bottle in there," he says. "Your favourite."

I squeal with delight. "Not Veuve?!" I ask, jumping up to peek in the minibar, where there is indeed a bottle of Veuve. I make a show of jumping up and down, my tits bouncing.

"Do that again," he growls. "But free your tits."

43

ADA

November 24, 2017

"I was driving home from work a couple of months since the last letter. I'd slackened off with getting security to walk me to the tram stop or to my car. It had started to seem over the top. Embarrassing. Self-important, when people had other things to do.

"I'd even slept with Ben a couple of times. Life was getting back to normal. My kind of normal. You were still worried—rightly, as it turned out. But I was just relieved. I wanted to forget about Kingston. I was...ashamed. That I'd made such a bad decision. I couldn't shake the revulsion with myself. That I got it so wrong."

Now I stop, chewing on my lip. I'd never said those words aloud before. I still feel an unbearable curling in my tummy when I think about Kingston. Not the kidnapping. Not the gun. Not even the sex. Or what came after.

Just my poor choices.

My poor judgement.

That somehow he'd gotten through.

All the therapy, all the words we applied to it—none of them had managed to shake that feeling of shame. I feel it in my body, all over. I can overlay it with the things I know to be true—but the feeling? It always comes a millisecond before.

It always comes first.

And it never goes away.

I hurry on, thinking of Ben.

"He was waiting in my car. He had a gun. I didn't even know he knew how to use one. He took me to his yacht. Had a bloody fancy table set up to woo me."

"Wait, wait. *What?*" Chloe has stopped looking all around us. She's staring at me in disbelief. But I hold a hand up, willing her to listen. We're standing on the footpath on Royal Parade, university students spilling out of campus opposite.

"Please, Chloe. I'll tell you the details later. I want to get back to Ben. Just let me finish. The short version."

She nods silently, her eyes wide.

"We drank two bottles of champagne. At least, Kingston thought we did. I had some sort of plan. By the time he'd banged me twice and I'd given him a lap dance, he wasn't watching what I did with my drink. He was drunk on joy as much as on champagne. So between spillages as we drunkenly groped each other and a couple of well-placed potted plants, much of my champagne didn't end up in my mouth."

To my surprise, Chloe is crying. Quietly. Tears roll down her cheeks. She's rocking her torso backwards and forwards, her mouth half open with silent sobs. Her eyes start darting around again.

"Just let me finish," I urge her. "I need you to understand this. Please, Chloe. Don't panic. It's okay. I'm okay."

I lead her to a low front garden wall and sit her on it, the rough bricks cutting into my thighs as I sit beside her. Wincing, I check her face, but she's just staring at me now, nodding, tears tracking down her cheeks. I expected panic. Rage. Hysteria.

I think I'm getting...empathy.

I hurry on.

"I didn't even end up making him chuck the gun. I was going for drunk, post-sex sleep. I never knew I had that in me. I played my role for four hours straight. It was bloody flawless. I thought about taking up acting afterwards," I deadpan at her, trying to lighten the mood, reassure her that I really am okay. I survived it. But Chloe doesn't even get close to a smile.

"So it...worked? And you got away? And you called the police...?" Her voice is shaky, hurried. "But then why—if he kidnapped you at gunpoint—why the fuck isn't he...? Why is he? How is he...more letters?" Her sentences are the most jumbled I've ever heard from her. They're interspersed with gasps and held-back sobs.

She goes to stand again, to pace no doubt, but I grab her hand and implore her to stay with me.

"I can't listen to this. I can't believe you had to do that. God, Ada," she starts to really sob. "I get it, you needed to escape. But I don't know how much more I can hear about this. Just tell me how it ended and let's get back to Ben." She's not looking at me, sitting hunched over, her shoulders shaking.

"It's bad, Chloe. Please. I need you to understand." I clutch at her hand, suddenly fearful. Of what she'll say. Of what she'll do.

"That was the worst part. The sex. Which might not make sense after you hear the rest of it. But giving my body to that jerk. Letting him feel so vindicated, so wonderful. Letting him touch me. Look at me. Kiss me. I fucking wanted to stab that fucker. I even thought about it."

I stop, thinking about that night, about what to say.

Kingston falling asleep, his arms wrapped tight around me.

The listing of the boat.

The warm yellow glow inside the tiny room.

The smell of sex, and sweat, and spilt champagne.

How dark it was outside.

I got up to pee, testing if he'd wake. He didn't even stir. And as

I slipped my clothes on, hurrying, starting to panic, not knowing where the fuck I was or how far I could get before he woke, I glanced at him and saw his eyes open.

To say I froze was an understatement.

I talked about this later with my therapist. I had never heard of it, but she told me that the well-known fight-flight response is actually not accurate. We have a fight-flight-freeze response. And people often freeze when they're being attacked. Later, they blame themselves.

Why didn't I fight back?

Why didn't I scream?

The legal system blames them too.

Why didn't you fight back?

Why didn't you scream?

There's no evidence of a struggle. Maybe because you consented? And felt bad later, for being so cheap?

Seconds passed, with me frozen to the spot. He didn't say a word. But then I remembered his unsettling quirk, sleeping with his eyes open.

The first few times it happened, I'd thought he was staring at me creepily in the dark. I'd startled, chattering away to him, frightened by his intense stare.

The next day, he remembered nothing.

It became a pattern. Particularly after drinking. So I remembered. I tethered my heart back inside my ribcage, grabbed my bag, and fled the boat.

On the pier, it was eerily quiet. Boats bobbed like ghouls in the water. One dim overhead light cast everything in a strange grey light.

For the amount of money floating on this tiny, overcrowded space, it sure as hell seemed ludicrously empty.

My heels clacked loudly on the boards—louder than I expected. I was torn between moving quickly and moving quietly. I didn't even know which direction I should be heading in.

Vaguely, I remembered the marina being a giant u-shape, with ten or twelve arms coming off one side. I hoped I was headed to the exit end of this arm—otherwise I'd have to go right back past Kingston's boat to get to the correct arm.

Either that or swim for it.

I could see the glow of the city lighting up the sky to the north, but I had no recollection of which way we came in, and I cursed my panic and lack of attention. *How are you supposed to save yourself if you don't pay attention to the exit?* I berated myself, reaching a t-intersection—which at least meant I took the correct turn the first time. But then I had the same problem. The right way would get me back to St Kilda. I think. *Would there be a locked gate at this time of the night?*

The wrong way would be a dead end.

I could see intermittent lights dotting along a line in both directions. One would be the pier to the beach; the other the wave attenuator. Squinting, I thought the one to my left looked more promising. I thought I could make out lights going all the way to the beach.

The boats creaked and clunked against their moorings. I strained to hear any movement above this. My heart was thudding in my chest.

Do I run or call the police?

If I can just get to the beach, there'll be people around, even in the middle of the night.

If I call the police, Kingston might hear me, and could certainly reach me before the police find their way out here. I didn't even know what the place was called, or if there was more than one yacht parking place in St Kilda.

I ran.

The thing about running though, is that once you start, you can no longer hear anything else.

Someone could be running behind you.

Or not.

And you can't stop to listen and check, in case they are.

I started to run, and all I could hear was my own breathing, the sound of my shoes, the wind against sails and rocks and waves.

I ran away from Kingston, and fear, and insanity, and danger.

And prostitution, maybe.

I sold my body for my life.

And still, two years later, looking at Chloe's devastated face, that's not the thing that makes my heart lurch.

My heart lurches about the fact that I made such a terrible, catastrophic mistake.

I ran as fast as I dared in heels, for as far as I could.

And then I couldn't run any more, because the path ended in the sea.

I'd taken the wrong turn.

Water stretched out before me, a good fifty metres of it between me and the wave attenuator. It looked dark and dangerous, reflecting back a million pieces of light, hiding shadows and secrets beneath its rolling waves.

Terror hit me a second behind nausea. It felt like adrenaline had surged through my body and out the other side, and my body was unable to process the aftermath. My stomach heaved in its wake. All I could hear was my gasping breath, a hair's breadth away from retching.

And all I could think was that if he was following me, I was trapped. There was nowhere else to run.

MY PHONE RINGING startles us both.

"Bill," I say, answering on the first ring.

"They've reset the fractures. He's still in a coma, but we can see him, one at a time. For a few minutes. I'm going in when they give me the okay."

"We're coming back," I tell him, ending the call, already standing and reaching for Chloe, relaying the message as we hurry back toward the hospital's main entrance.

"What the fuck happened on the pier, Ada? Give me the abridged version. You've got about three minutes."

44

ADA – 34 YEARS OLD

EARLY MORNING ON OCTOBER 25, 2014

I looked at the sea, and I looked at the pier.

It was maybe two hundred metres to the beach. I was an accomplished swimmer; two hundred metres, even in open sea, should be manageable. The swell was restless, but not huge.

It seemed less terrifying than going back past the pier arm that housed Kingston's boat. Kingston. He was drunk, but would he stir? Reach for me, and find me gone?

I felt close to vomiting. My whole body was shaking. Maybe I wouldn't even be able to run, let alone swim.

Seconds dragged by as I weighed my options.

Swim, I decided.

I would take it slow.

I pulled off my heels and started to climb down the rocky side of the pier. It was wet and dark, difficult to make out the shapes of the boulders, what was a gaping hollow and what was solid rock. Sharp edges cut into my feet. My heart still pounded in my ears.

And then a strong hand reached out and grabbed me.

Everything happened very quickly after that.

His grip was vice-like, despite the Veuve.

Instinctively, I reared backwards, wrenching away from him, more from shock than any plan to loosen his grip.

But he was leaning over the edge. So as I pulled backwards, he lost his balance.

For a moment he held onto me, rather than trying to break his fall. Then his grip left my arm.

He fell head first into the rocks below me, right where they met the water, his legs pointing back up to the pier. His body was twisted toward me, his arms still outstretched upwards, reflecting his indecision about whether to hold on to me or break his fall. His skin glowed pale and strange in the low light.

He didn't move.

And even as I watched, he slid slowly, slowly down the incline.

Just another few inches.

Just enough for his face to disappear beneath the lapping waves.

I'D LIKE to say I didn't think. That panic drove me into the water. The two hundred metres subsequently covered, fully clothed, lost from my memory amongst the fear and the adrenaline and the sheer horror of the night.

But I did think.

I carried my heels with me instead of discarding them in the water, as I'd intended to do when I made the decision to swim. Before an arm reached out and grabbed me.

I chose to swim, rather than try to find my way out of the marina, risk there being locked gates or other people.

When I got to the shore, exhausted, freezing despite the summer night, I didn't call for help. My phone, my whole handbag was drenched. But I had held on to it. I was not leaving it at the scene.

And when a young, drunk couple on the beach asked if I was all right, I told them a creepy guy had chased me on the marina, and I'd swum to get away from him.

They offered me a towel, which I gratefully accepted. But when they offered to call the police, I waved them off, already looking around to get my bearings.

At least I had remembered where I'd parked the car.

Civic duty, they said, calling anyway. *He'll probably look for another victim.* But by the time they turned back to me, having given the scant details to the police, I had sprinted down a side street and was long gone.

By the time the police got to the scene, I hoped like hell that Kingston would be too.

I didn't kill Kingston.

But I didn't save him, either.

45

ADA

November 24, 2017

When I finally see Ben, a small cry escapes my lips.

He's lying on his back, a small tube coming out of his head and feeding into scary-looking medical equipment. His scalp is shaved around it. Tubes feed into his nose and mouth. Ugly bruises bloom across his face.

One leg is in some sort of brace from his ankle to his crotch, suspended slightly above the bed. Tubes and needles seem to run in every direction.

Machines whir and flash beside him.

Bill had tried to prepare me, but he had failed.

I creep toward him, the chair Bill recently vacated still warm, Ben's hand resting on the bed covers right in front of me. Tentatively, I touch the back of it with my fingertips.

"Ben, Ben," I whisper, my voice catching, the tears starting to roll down my cheeks.

The thought of Ben in pain is crucifying me.

But the thought of my life without him is what's killing me.

BACK IN THE WAITING ROOM, Janey is still quietly comforting Bill. I've never seen her relinquish centre stage for so long in my life.

To my surprise, Chloe is still there too, sitting off to one side, scrolling on her phone.

She looks up when I walk in.

"Can I see him?" she asks, and I shake my head.

"A nurse kicked me out. Said visiting hours are over. And that he needs to rest. I'm sorry, Chloe; I didn't realise you were waiting... I should have realised."

She brushes me away. "It's your place, love," she says softly, and I feel my cheeks heat again.

I shoot her an angry glance, and she frowns.

"Really, Ada? He's unconscious, and you're going to stick with the stepsister role?" Her voice is low but incredulous. I can't believe she's going to do this here, now.

"Really, Chloe?" I hiss. "He's unconscious, and you're going to make me deal with that, too?"

She glares at me for a moment, then seems to relent.

"They're not listening," she says, resigned. "This conversation isn't over, but maybe now isn't the time. I'm going to go home."

The thought of her leaving makes me feel panicky. We haven't spoken about that night on the pier. What I did.

What I didn't do.

What happens now.

"Don't go yet," I say, my heart thumping. I need something from her. To know what she's going to do with the information?

Absolution, maybe?

"What about what we spoke about?" I ask her, my voice low.

Chloe looks at me thoughtfully. "What about it?"

"Well, what happens now?"

"I've been googling. I'm confused as to why you just didn't tell us he was dead when you got the first letter."

My eyes snap up to hers.

"He's definitely dead?"

Chloe stares at me.

"Yessss," she says slowly, looking at me curiously. "I found a couple of articles. Did you never read them?"

I shake my head, my eyes wide. I reach for her phone.

"Wait," she says, not yet relinquishing it. "What did you do that night? The next day? The day after? You didn't tell any of us... Did you go to the police?"

I shake my head, looking into her eyes, pleading with her to understand.

For once, she doesn't leap to judgement and hysteria.

She pats the seat next to her instead.

"I don't understand" is all she says.

How to explain? I know it doesn't make any sense. I know it's unforgivable.

"I panicked," I tell her, my voice still low. "I left him, Chloe. I wanted him to die that night. I hated myself for letting him into our lives. I hated myself for going along with his stupid fantasy of getting back together. I hated how badly I had misjudged everything. I wanted to pretend it never happened."

"But weren't you terrified that he was still alive, and that he'd come after you? Or that the police would look into it, and find your DNA all over his boat?"

"Yes. I worked from home for a couple of weeks. But I also thought, those kids called the police. There was a report of a creepy guy chasing a woman along the pier, and she was so frightened she swam for it. So the police would have found him if he was still in the water. I hoped they would think he slipped on the rocks trying to grab and rape someone. And got his just desserts. And it probably sounds stupid, but I thought if I was googling his name, that if they did come after me, it would make it look like I knew something. If they checked my computer...or something."

"But if they found evidence of sex and champagne in his boat, they would have known he had a woman there, earlier at least. They would surely want to find her for questioning."

"I wasn't thinking, okay!" My voice is too loud, and Bill and Janey both glance over at us. I drop my voice again, battle the tears that are threatening to spill again. I rub at my eyes angrily.

"I was ashamed. Of all of it. Of every single thing to do with Kingston. I still am," I say, my voice flat, resigned.

To my surprise, Chloe doesn't say anything. Instead she takes my hand and rests her head on my shoulder. And we just sit like that, for a while.

46

ADA

November 25, 2017

When I wake the next morning, my whole body aches.

The nurses had encouraged us to go find a motel, advising that Ben was unlikely to wake overnight, but Bill, Janey, and I had stayed in the waiting room anyway. Now, my phone says 6:52 a.m., and I think that they were right. I feel terrible, and it's unlikely to improve any time soon.

After Chloe went home the night before, I'd googled.

Man found dead on pier, *The Age* states on Sunday, October 27, 2015.
In the early hours of Saturday, October 24th, an unnamed man was found deceased on the marina of the Royal Melbourne Yacht Squadron. Police cite cause of death as drowning following a head injury. The deceased, in his late thirties, is believed to moor his yacht on the marina and to have been entertaining on his boat earlier that night.
Police are asking for any witnesses or anyone with information to call Crime Stoppers...

Another article—on Friday, October 30, 2015:

Deceased man named as Melbourne millionaire, Kingston Berry.

Berry was found dead on the marina of the Royal Melbourne Yacht Squadron in the early hours of Saturday, October 24th. He is believed to have drowned after slipping on the rocks and sustaining a head injury. He had a blood alcohol level of 0.21. A witness left the beach around the time of death after speaking to a couple who provided her with a towel. Police are asking she come forward to assist them in their enquiries. She is not a suspect. She is described as medium height, with long auburn hair. She was wearing a white shirt and black skirt and appeared to have been swimming in the vicinity.

I couldn't find anything else, and I'd lain across some bench seats and tried to sleep, the lights and noise and worries constantly waking me.

I glance across at Janey and Bill, who are both sitting quietly. Bill notices that I'm awake and smiles wanly. "No news," he offers, before I can open my mouth.

I nod, reaching for my bag. "I'll get coffee," I say, and he nods in thanks.

When I come back, they're speaking to a nurse, and my heart rate picks up as I hurry over.

"They're moving him to the ward," Bill tells me. That this is good news is clear on his face. He turns back to the nurse. "So we can visit after ten?"

She nods, then moves away.

"He's still unconscious, but stable. Now we just have to wait to see how he is when he wakes up," Bill tells me. I hand them both coffees and sit beside Mum. Then I stand back up.

"I'll let Chloe know," I say.

I step out into the Mooroop Wa-Lam-Buk Garden, which is

surprisingly busy considering the time, to make the call. Bright morning sunshine and some greenery is a welcome change after the fluorescent lights in the waiting area.

"I'll come in a bit later," Chloe tells me, after I've updated her on Ben. Not that there's much to update. "But I actually wanted to say something to you."

I brace myself. There's been so much over the last twenty-four hours that I don't know if I can cope with much more.

Chloe, telling Mum about Ben and me.

Ben shouting at me, then being hit by a car.

Reliving that night with Kingston on the pier. Telling somebody what happened for the first time.

Seeing Ben, all broken up. The unsettled feeling that came with the fear and the shock. The feeling that there's something else I've gotten wrong, that I can't quite put my finger on.

"Yes?" I say carefully, feeling on edge. Feeling close to tears again.

"What we were talking about in the taxi. That conversation between Mum and Dawn."

"Okay?" I say.

"I just wanted to say—seriously—if that conversation between Mum and Dawn twenty years ago is all you've based your decision on about not being with Ben, you're a fucking idiot."

Her tone is mild, but the sentiment is not. And it seems simplistic and infuriating.

"When you say it like that, of course it sounds stupid," I snap. "But I took it as a warning. Not to get any ideas. That she wouldn't accept it."

"She was cackling away with Dawn because of who Dawn was married to. All the lewd comments about stepbrothers? Dawn was married to her stepbrother. I remember overhearing them one night."

"You mean eavesdropping," I interject, unable to help myself.

Chloe's habit of sitting on the stair landing and listening in on adult conversations was a favourite pastime of hers.

"Whatever," she says. "Are you listening to me? *Mum does not give a flying fuck.*"

I open my mouth to argue—well why didn't anyone say anything if it was so fine and everyone's known forever, or something like that—when Chloe continues.

"You know what I think, Ada? I think that's an excuse. I think that's the reason you've told yourself all this time, because it puts the blame on somebody else. And it means you don't have to make that choice yourself. And that choice? I think you'd make the same one. Not because you don't want to be with Ben, but because it's not nice and shiny and perfect enough for you. You busy yourself with this perfect life. You run the best magazine. You keep yourself all pretty and presentable. You are the best at everything you do. You read all the right newspapers and support all the right issues. You're the best company, if you deign to grant us with your presence. Your business instincts are spot-on. You do the 'right thing' on every occasion. But marrying your stepbrother? That would be a big fucking blip on your perfect record. Because *you* think it's a bit wrong. You and your bloody perfect standards. Which is probably why you liked Kingston in the first place. He ticked all the boxes that would make everyone approve. Handsome, rich, got along with everyone. Until he turned out to be a lunatic, that is."

By the time she finishes, I can hear her breathing. I can't quite tell if she's furious or frustrated. On the occasions I tried to interject, her voice just rose a few octaves, warning me off it, her feelings seeming to grow as she spoke—about something I don't quite understand.

"How can you say that to me?" I whisper, tears pricking my eyes again. God, this crying business is getting out of hand at the moment. "After everything I told you last night?"

Her voice softens. "Yeah. I think they're linked together, Adds.

You chose Kingston without your good judgement. Because he wasn't Ben. But that's really where your judgement failed. On deciding Ben wasn't the right thing to do. Kingston, and everything that came with him, was just collateral damage. You're beating yourself up about choosing him, when you should be looking at why you didn't choose Ben."

Now *I* feel furious.

"I didn't choose Ben because you were all against it," I hiss, though even as I say it, I realise that I have no evidence for that. Chloe's refusal to talk about it and my belief Mum would go nuts about it are hardly evidence that everyone would reject me over it.

"Are you sure?" she asks, her voice suddenly gentle. And a sob escapes me. Because I'm not. And I don't know what that means.

"Aren't you shocked about what happened?" I whisper, ignoring her question, conscious of people all around me. Not used to crying in public.

"I think you did exactly what you needed to do, Ada," she says gently. "I don't give two fucks about your duty of care. The guy kidnapped you at gunpoint. I don't know how you got through the last two years without sharing what you went through. I almost can't believe how strong you are, except I can. You're the strongest, most determined person that I know. But I think you're lying to yourself about Ben. I think you need to have a pretty good think about that. 'Cause he's going to need support when he wakes up. You might want to be pretty clear about where you fit into that.

"But Kingston? I have no absolutely no problem with that fucker ending up dead."

After we hang up—Chloe's shift to being an insightful sister both comforting and confronting to me—I sit in the garden for a while and think about what she said.

She's wrong, as it happens.

Because thinking about it: I don't care if people think I'm perfect, or good, or bad, or mediocre.

All my hard work, getting everything right—that's not for other people. It's not to seek their validation or approval or anything else.

All this winning? All this perfection?

That's to convince *myself* that I'm okay.

47

ADA

I'M SITTING by Ben's bed, holding his hand, turning it over gently in mine. Stroking his palm and running my fingertips along the length of his elegant fingers.

I can't look at him as I talk, even though he's unconscious and unable to judge me.

Bill had ushered me in first today. It's still morning, the conversation with Chloe fresh in my mind, the conversation with my therapist less so. There's something elusive about my thoughts. I just can't quite get them to match up to my feelings.

Is Bill thinking of me as his son's girlfriend or his son's stepsister? I wonder to myself.

"Chloe tells me that Mum knows about us being together," I continue, stealing a glance at Ben's eyes. They remain closed. It's hard to tell if he's at peace or in pain through all the bandaging and tubes. I guess he's probably on good drugs. "So you'll be pleased to know that you were right all along. Apparently, she must not care. I haven't had the courage to say anything to her though."

I feel silly talking to an unconscious person. And

embarrassed at the thought that a nurse might walk in and hear me. But it's more important that Ben knows that I'm here.

"I can't really make sense of it. Why she wouldn't have said anything. And Bill is certainly looking at me strangely all of a sudden, which doesn't fit in with them knowing for years. Anyway. I'll worry about that another day."

I hesitate, watching his face for signs that he can hear me, that he's listening. But he's very still. His hand is limp in mine.

"You shouted at me yesterday at work. I think you were coming to tell me that Chloe had told Mum about us. She told me you visited her. She was really touched you were so caring, so crushed about the miscarriages for her. So I'm guessing that's why you came, why you called me so many times. And I think you thought I had some other guy with me. You've never shouted at me like that before. Not really. Not meaning it."

I think about Ben being angry with me. Not talking to me. My heart lurches painfully in my chest.

"It was just Chloe I was shouting at. I was so angry she'd told Mum. I threw the phone against the wall. She pushed everything off my desk. It was real, actual breakage. It was kind of satisfying." I smile a little bit. "I think you'd find that funny, if you were awake. My office finally saw some real temper."

I'm silent for a while, not sure what to say. Eventually, I clutch his hand tighter.

"The doctors say you took a pretty hard hit to the head. They're worried about brain damage. They've done some scans, and everything looks okay. But you had some swelling. They had to operate. And they said we just have to wait until you wake up to check how you are."

I stop, struggling with tears again.

"Please be okay, Ben. Please. I can bear anything if you're okay. Not having you is the only thing I can't bear." I start to sob: saying the words aloud, voicing my fears, my feelings—I know I'm right. Mum's wrath is nothing compared to not having Ben in my life.

And somehow, all the stress of the last few days, Kingston, everything held in for so long comes spewing out of me. My eyes, really. My eyes and mouth and nose.

I sit in the quiet room, and sob and shake and curse myself.

Because if I'd never broken up with him, he'd never have been so excited to come tell me that Mum knew, that there was no barrier to us being together.

If I'd answered his calls, instead of shouting at Chloe, he wouldn't have left in anger.

And if he wasn't so angry and hurt, maybe he would have been paying more attention to the road. And not stepped out in front of that fucking car.

"I'm sorry. I'm so sorry, Ben. About everything. About not believing in us. For breaking up with you. For not answering your calls yesterday. For not seeing that you're the most important one. You're the one person I should stop everything for. You're the one person who always believes in me, who always says and does exactly the right thing. I'm sorry it's taken me so long to realise it. And you have to be okay. You have to be okay so I can tell you that when you can hear it and say 'I told you so.'"

I'm still sobbing when Bill knocks gently on the door.

Hurriedly, I try to compose myself.

"Can I see him for a while, love?" he asks, looking down at the door handle with excessive interest to give me a moment.

God, he's a nice guy.

"Of course," I say, rising, wiping the back of my hands across my eyes. "I'll go sit with Mum."

"She's gone home for a little while," he says, stopping me at the door, tucking stray hair behind my ears. Pulling me into a hug. Then he pats me awkwardly on the back and goes to take my chair.

I wander around the food court, but can't muster up any appetite. I can't stop thinking about what Chloe said.

Because she was close, I realise. She was nearly right.

But not quite.

BACK IN THE WAITING ROOM, ushered away from Ben for the daily rest period, Bill and I sit quietly together. We're both nursing coffees and sombre expressions.

Eventually, shifting uncomfortably in his seat, Bill starts the conversation that I've been dreading.

"So, witnesses say that Ben didn't look and stepped out on the road against the 'don't walk' sign. So I don't think it sounds like Kingston had anything to do with this. But that last letter...well... it could be read as a bit of a threat. I just wanted to talk about that."

He looks studiously at his coffee cup, one finger circling the lid, not wanting to embarrass me. I can feel my face burning. I feel like I'm going to throw up. Again. I reach out a hand to clutch my chair, the coffee churning uncomfortably in my empty stomach.

"It's okay, Adds," Bill goes on quickly, stealing a glance at me. "I know you're embarrassed. I know you've never wanted to tell us. But you don't need to be worried on our account. It's maybe time to get that out in the open, don't you think? Especially now. If it might be connected. And if Ben needs you."

I choke back a sob. I don't know whether I'm going to throw up or howl. I can't look at Bill, and I want to run away.

Not deal with this.

Not now.

Not ever.

But why? If he doesn't seem to care?

In the end, I feel too sick to move. I slump in my chair, hiding my face in my hands, and cry quietly.

Not just because we're having this conversation and I'm mortified.

But also because of all the mistakes I've made. They're piling up in front of me, inescapable. And I just can't quite compute that I've gotten so many things so wrong. When I put so much effort into getting everything right.

Bill puts down his coffee and tentatively reaches over to rub my back. His touch is gentle and warm. And surprisingly comforting.

"I don't know why you don't want to tell us, love. It's not really any of my business. But for what it's worth, I'd be delighted if you were my daughter-in-law as well as my stepdaughter. I don't care what anyone thinks, but even if they care, I don't. You and Ben are two of the best people I know. If you're happy, I'm happy. So please...don't cry about that."

"I didn't think Mum would accept it," I choke out, wondering why it's so much easier to talk to Bill than to my own mother. "She always seems to care an awful lot what people think."

Bill fidgets with his coffee cup some more. I sneak a sideways glance at him. He looks pensive.

"Your mum is certainly a complex woman," he says eventually, his expression unreadable. Then he glances at me, looking serious. "I know she's not the most attentive mum. She does try, in her own way."

I find that very hard to believe, but I admire Bill's loyalty, so I don't tell him so. I could never quite work them out. They seem to have completely different styles and values. But Bill looks content and full of warmth talking about my mother. Conscious of her mothering flaws, maybe...but genuinely happy in his marriage nonetheless.

He bumps shoulders with me gently. "It's not as big a deal as you think it is," he says.

We're silent for a few minutes. I'm trying to digest this information, on top of all the other surprises of the last two days. But after some more fidgeting, Bill moves the conversation on. "So. About Kingston. What do you think?"

I startle.

I'd forgotten about Kingston.

Glancing at Bill then hurriedly away, now it's my turn to fidget with my coffee cup.

"Chloe and I just googled him. He's actually dead. For a couple of years, I think." I continue to studiously examine my cup. "I don't know why I didn't think to do that earlier."

Bill looks confused. "Why didn't the police tell Chloe that when she took in the letter?" Then, the question that I've been wrestling with: "And if he's dead...then...who's sending these letters?"

I look at him, shrug, look away. "I doubt the police even looked him up. They would have looked at those letters and shooed her away in minutes, I imagine. The first one was essentially a friend request. The second one wasn't threatening." I blush again. *Unless you read it as a threat to out us, I suppose*, I think to myself. "And as for the letters...I don't know. They're quite different to the ones Kingston sent years ago. So I'm not sure that someone is trying to pretend they're him. Or who would want to do that. Or why... But they don't really make any sense. The first one must be someone I've dated, wanting to stay in touch, telling me how happy they are... They sound like they're trying to make me jealous, maybe? Except, I haven't really dated anyone else. And the second one..." My voice trails off. Who else would send the second one, except a jealous lover?

We sit in silence again. Surprisingly, it's comfortable. I'm glad it's just Bill and me talking about this.

Thank God I ended up with one relatively normal parent, I think to myself.

Bill shifts in his seat, and I find him looking at me, his face worried. "It seems to me like it's still someone trying to hurt you in some way, Ada."

I nod, looking away. That's pretty much the same conclusion

that I've come to. But before I can answer him, one of the doctors hurries over to us, and my stomach lurches.

Ben.

"Good news," she says, offering her hand as she looks at both of us in turn. "He's awake. He's pretty groggy and dozing off and on, not really saying anything yet, but everything looks good so far. You'll be able to go in and see him in about fifteen. I'll come by a bit later to see how he is."

She hurries off, and Bill and I look at each other and grin—shaky, relieved smiles. Then inexplicably, I start to cry again.

"Bloody hell," I mutter. And Bill pulls me against him, patting my hair, shushing me gently.

"It's been a big couple of days, love. It's okay to cry."

The fact that he actually sees me, and what this all means to me, just makes me cry harder. It's in stark contrast to Mum's oblivion.

But then again, I haven't gotten everything right either, I remind myself.

I thought I knew Mum so well, knew exactly how she'd react to me dating my stepbrother. And apparently I was so far off the mark I didn't even notice that she already knew.

What does that say about my judgement? I wonder to myself.

48

ADA

THE NEXT FIFTEEN minutes pass excruciatingly slowly.

We hover in the ward near the nurses' station, waiting for 2:30 p.m. to arrive. Itching to see Ben.

Just short of then, a nurse beckons us over, smiling warmly. "Nice for him to see some friendly faces when he wakes up," she says, ushering us into his room.

The tube has been removed from his skull, replaced by a rectangular bandage. His beautiful hair has been shaved off around it. Dark stubble lines his jaw, and dark bruising blooms across his face and skull.

His eyes are closed, but they flutter as the nurse fusses around him, chatting to him brightly.

Bill ushers me into the chair next to the bed, his hand on the small of my back. "Go on, love," he says, his voice husky. "Reckon your face might be the one he most wants to see."

"Dad." Ben's voice is barely audible. His eyes stay closed.

"Yeah, mate. I'm here. Gave us a bloody fright, you did. How are you feeling?"

Ben just sighs, his head rolling slightly to the side.

"He'll be drifting in and out of sleep for a little while as the sedatives wear off," the nurse explains, checking various pieces of medical equipment around him. "Press the button when he wakes if I'm not here," she says, indicating a button on the cord hanging on the head of the bed. "The doctor will want to see him."

We nod at her and she leaves the room.

Tentatively, I squeeze Ben's hand. This time, his fingers curl slightly into mine and hold on.

An hour passes. Bill and I alternate sitting next to Ben. He stirs a few times but doesn't wake.

Finally, he opens his eyes, and after a few moments they focus on Bill.

"Dad," he murmurs. "I dreamt you were here."

"Not a dream, buddy. We've been hanging around for a day or two."

"We?" Ben goes to look around, and winces.

"All of us. Chloe and Janey have gone home now. Just Ada and me holding the fort."

"Ada." I can't hear anything in his tone. Happy? Angry? I hurry into his line of vision so he doesn't try to move again.

"I'm just going to go let the nurse know you're awake, buddy. I think they want to check you out, make sure the old noggin' is working the way it should. You had a good whack to the head." Bill squeezes Ben's hand, then moves out of the room. To give us a moment, I have no doubt, eyeing the button the nurse told us to press.

I sit down next to him, reaching for his hand, searching his eyes. Suddenly worried I'm going to start crying again.

"Good to see you," he murmurs, squeezing my hand.

"You too," I mutter. Not sure where to start. Not sure what I want to say.

"It was just Chloe," I blurt out. "At the office. You yelled at me."

Ben frowns, struggling to sit up, but grimaces and slumps back down.

"Mmmm," he says, closing his eyes again.

"Premature," I smile at the nurse uncertainly when she returns with Bill. "He's out again. He knew me, though."

"That's a great sign." She nods at me encouragingly. "He should stay awake a bit longer each time. Just grab me again next time."

Bill and I look at each other.

We keep on waiting.

———

CHLOE COMES IN SHORTLY AFTERWARDS, and after she's popped in to see Ben, who hasn't woken again, we go for another walk around the block.

I feel stiff and exhausted. Though the nurse and doctor were both positive, until I hear Ben say something clever and irreverent, I won't feel sure that he's okay.

More than okay.

That he's his normal, beautiful, perfect self.

Chloe doesn't beat around the bush.

"Are you going to tell Ben about Kingston?"

Another question I've thought about and thought about and have no answer to.

"I guess that depends. There's a lot to sort out. I don't know where we stand or what's going to happen. I think I need to deal with one thing at a time."

"Like what?"

I think about that. I don't really want to talk about it.

Like, are Ben and I going to be together now? Is it that easy?

Like, how did I manage to misjudge Mum's reaction so monumentally about this?

Like, who is sending these latest letters? Who wants to upset me? And why would they deliver a letter to Chloe's house? Frankly, there aren't enough people in my life to warrant two stalkerish correspondents. One, surely, should be enough for a hermit like me?

Not to mention my obsession with getting everything just right, which is irking Jason, scaring my employees, inspiring out-of-character wisdom in Chloe, and failing anyway. And has maybe stopped me from getting the very thing I want most, for all these years.

In trying to get everything just right, have I actually managed to get everything completely wrong?

"Ada?"

"What?"

"What do you mean, what?"

"Sorry. I wasn't listening."

Chloe blows out her breath loudly, exasperated. "Did you think at all about what I said yesterday?"

"Yes. There's something in what you said. But it's not quite right. I'm trying to untangle it," I tell her. "In the meantime...any ideas about who else might be sending me creepy letters?"

Chloe frowns.

"No." She pauses for a minute, both of us thinking.

Neither of us have anything to add.

BY THE TIME visiting hours are over, Ben has woken a couple more times and chatted briefly to Bill, Chloe, and me as well as the nurses and doctor.

Nothing of significance has been discussed between us, but the general medical opinion is that everything is going as well as can be expected. There are no concerning symptoms, though we have been advised to monitor for a whole heap of possible warning signs, including emotional changes, aggression, slow speech or processing speed. Not that's he's leaving the hospital any time soon.

Bill and I are both shattered by the time we leave the hospital. I can't believe it's only Saturday night. It was only yesterday that Chloe confessed to telling Janey my second best kept secret; that Ben left my office and was hit by car; and I told Chloe about my actual *very* best kept secret—the first person I had ever told.

I feel like I've aged ten years.

The trip home seems to take forever. Then I crawl straight into bed and fall into an exhausted sleep.

49

ADA

When I finally get to talk to Ben alone, I just bloody cry again.

"Tell me," Ben says, his eyes half closed, his bed reclined. He looks exhausted, too.

"Not now," I sniff. "You need to rest."

"I can't rest if you don't tell me why you're crying. I'll worry instead of rest. You'll be doing me harm, actually," he says, managing a slight smile. "If you want me to get better, you'd better start talking."

He's trying to make light of things, to make me feel okay—about sitting here crying, about Friday, about everything. It only makes me cry more.

"I've made so many mistakes," I mutter eventually.

"We all do."

"No. Not me. I don't. I get things right. That's who I am."

Ben opens his eyes wider and looks at me thoughtfully. He presses a button and his bed starts to move upright. He stops it part way, wincing.

"Why? Why is that so important to you? Mistakes are how we learn things. Why is making a mistake so unacceptable to you? A mistake doesn't mean you're a bad person. Even your worst mistake doesn't mean you're a bad person. We're more than even our worst mistake."

I can't explain this to him; I don't even understand it myself.

"Are you worried that people will think less of you?" he asks eventually.

"No," I say scornfully, frowning at him. "Do you know me at all?"

He grins, the hand I'm clutching suddenly pulling me into him, his other arm finding the back of my neck.

"Yes. Yes, I believe I do," he says, pulling me closer, leaning in to kiss my neck. The way I like him to. The way that makes me feel weak and dizzy with longing.

I push away from him, smiling despite myself. "Don't start something you're not prepared to finish," I tell him, looking meaningfully at his leg.

"Oh, I can finish, sweetheart," he tells me, smirking. "You just might have to do all the work." He lies back, wriggling his hips suggestively. Then he winces and closes his eyes.

"Huh," I say, raising my eyebrows at him, but his eyes remain closed.

"So tell me."

I frown. Inexplicably, I feel a sense of shame creeping over me. How can I tell him something I don't even know myself?

"Just try," he says. "Sometimes talking about it can help you figure it out. Plus, I'm a captive audience. You could bore me with your internal monologue for days and I can't escape, even if I wanted to."

"My internal monologue is never boring," I tell him, deadpan, and he opens his eyes and looks at me with his head tilted back, resting on the pillows.

"I bet," he whispers. Then: "I missed you." For a while, I think he's drifted off to sleep, but eventually he squeezes my hand.

"So tell me about these mistakes."

I'm silent for a while. How can I share these things with Ben? I feel like, without my protective armour, I might turn into a wisp of smoke and float away. That the world might actually come crashing down around my ears. Something. Something bad and unexpected. Because the truth is, I've never been any other way.

"Chloe thinks I can't bear to make mistakes because I want everyone to think I'm marvellous. But that's not right. I don't care about that. I care...about how it makes *me* feel. It makes me feel ashamed. Like a mistake is more global than the one action or inaction that it represents. That making a mistake is all of me. That *I'm* the mistake. That *I'm* not good enough."

We sit like this for a while, our fingers intertwined, Ben's eyes closed.

"Tell me about one," he says, just when I think he really can't think of anything to say. "So you can see that my opinion of you won't change because you made a mistake."

"You don't know that," I whisper. "You don't know what they are."

Ben opens his eyes and looks straight at me. "I've known you for twenty-three years, Miss Cosgrove," he says. "There is nothing you could say or do that would make me love you any less."

Sure, I think to myself. Letting errors slip through in the magazine, *that* type of mistake isn't going to change how he sees me—but what about leaving a man to die? What about a sex marathon with him in order to escape?

Start smaller, I tell myself. I want to believe Ben more than I want to believe anything in the world is true. But all these mistakes together feel too big, too painful, too messed up.

"Well...there's Kingston," I say slowly. "I just can't forgive myself for my poor judgement. That I let someone so unhinged into my life. Into our whole family's lives. I thought I was a good judge of character. And every time I think about it I actually feel sick. And it's not that he became so creepy and scary. It's that I *chose the wrong person*—that's what makes me feel sick."

"I was coming to tell you that Chloe told Janey about us," Ben says suddenly.

"Are you listening to me?" I ask.

"Yes." He smiles. "I just wanted to throw that out there. That Janey doesn't care. To make sure you know."

"Chloe was telling me when you came to the office. The shouting. I was throwing things at her."

"I dreamt you said that. It felt like it was true."

"I did say that. When you first came to."

"Right," he says, smiling, gripping my hand. "I'm sorry I shouted at you. I thought..."

"I know," I tell him, clutching his hand fiercely. "I'm sorry. I should have answered the phone. I was so angry with her..." I trail off. Another mistake. "So I was wrong about Mum too. Losing her shit. I spent so much time worrying about it. I made decisions based on my belief. I never checked." *I nearly lost you,* I want to say, but I don't know if I still might lose him. I don't know if he'll still love me after I tell him all of this.

"Fixable," Ben says, looking at me through half-closed eyes. "That mistake is fixable." His intensity is palpable, even looking half asleep.

"There's more," I whisper, looking down.

"Okay," he says, his voice gentle, inviting. Like he's standing by his declaration—he really believes there's nothing I can say to change how he feels about me.

"Chloe thinks it's part of wanting everyone to think I'm so fucking wonderful—that I couldn't bear the shame of dating my stepbrother. That it would tarnish my image. And it's close to that. I can't quite put my finger on it." I fall into silence, and Ben waits, quiet too.

"You know, I saw a therapist for a while after Kingston. I wasn't entirely honest with her about what happened. But we talked a lot about the rules I hold myself to. Like, 'I must never make mistakes' and 'the job is not done unless it's perfect.' And we spoke about where that might have come from, which you know already. Always trying to get Mum's attention. And never succeeding, so trying harder and harder. And that perhaps that has just become a way of life. I know in my mind there's more important things, but in the moment, it's like white noise. All I can focus on is that next thing that needs doing. So socialising, pursuing hobbies...it all seems like a waste of time. I can't enjoy it. It makes me claustrophobic. I'm always thinking about all the things I need to do. And work became a way to channel that, I suppose. And that's okay. That's just how I work. I'm okay with that. More than okay. I *enjoy* work."

I'm silent for a while, untangling pieces of the puzzle as I try to articulate them. Then: "I think it became a way to convince myself that I was okay. If I could do everything right, win at everything, then I could say—*see?! I'm okay! I'm just fine!* Not to everyone else. Not even to Mum. Just to myself. Like if I did enough of the right things, I'd feel good about myself too.

"My therapist said that this is protective, it was probably the way I coped when Mum couldn't give me what I needed. And now it's just habitual. I don't know how to undo it. It feels *good* to me. I like doing everything just right. I go to bed happy and satisfied. But now...with all these things unravelling...it's like I don't know who I am. Like somehow my self-esteem has always rested on that. And I feel kind of...*erased*..."

Ben squeezes my hand gently. "So it helped you cope. It's been useful. But now...it's interfering with things? Like us?"

"I don't know," I say, frowning. "When I think about it, I don't know why I've been so hung up on the stepbrother thing. It suddenly seems...irrational. Especially with you..." My voice trails off as I look at Ben's bruises, his broken body. Right on cue, he winces as he tries to shift in the bed.

"Do you need anything? Pain meds?"

He shakes his head. "What did your therapist say about undoing it? That need to get everything right?"

"Well...we ran into a few problems with that." I shift uncomfortably in my seat. The truth was, I just stopped going to therapy. I didn't actually see a problem with the way I was. "She wanted me to think about whether these rules were realistic, and think about the negative consequences of them. And maybe rework the rules. Make different decisions based on the new rules."

"And?"

"And...I quit therapy at about that point. I couldn't see any negative consequences. And I think she was going for the idea that it wasn't realistic, and I would feel devastated when I did make a mistake or didn't live up to the standards I set for myself. Which turns out to be true. But at the time, I thought—I did meet those standards. I always met them. I didn't know what she was talking about. Like, that was the whole point, right? I *did* meet my standards. What she was saying just didn't make any sense to me. It didn't seem *relevant*. I thought she was talking about everyone else. Everyone with less discipline. Those people who would set a bar and never reach it. That had never happened to me. I set the bar high, and I cleared it every time."

Ben sits quietly, waiting.

"And now...I'm confused. I feel like I've gotten a lot of things wrong. I just feel...like it hasn't worked out the way I expected it to. Things have...splattered."

"Splattered?" Ben is raising one eyebrow at me, attentive and curious, despite his discomfort. Like he really wants to understand...but at the same time, he manages to convey adoration.

"I think the idea of mistakes...I think I've got it all back to front. It's like," I stop, look at the ceiling. For once, I'm not being avoidant. I'm trying to work out the sentences that will match these thoughts, these feelings. This sense that I got it all so very, very wrong. "Even us, you know? The sex? The crazy games I made up."

"The *hot* games you made up," Ben corrects me, his gaze on me steady and warm and accepting.

"But even that...it wasn't *real*. I put so much thought and effort into that, like everything else, because I wanted to be the best lay you ever had, the most fun in bed, and yes I enjoyed it too...but it seems kind of pathetic and exhausting in retrospect. That I didn't think you'd like me just for me. So I even *researched* it, for God's sake. Before that first time? I didn't just plan it. I read books, and looked at magazines, and tried to work out what was sexy, and what you'd like. So I didn't experience it as this special thing that was happening between us. I feel like I...missed out on that. And like I missed this major, major thing about myself."

"You were pursuing perfection not to prove to other people that you were okay," Ben says, staring at me. "You were trying to prove it to yourself. You didn't feel good about yourself and you buried it so far under achieving things that you didn't even know it."

And as he says the words, I feel a crushing pain in my chest, an explosion of lightness and weight, of pain and fear and wonder. Because that niggling sense, that worry that I couldn't articulate, couldn't work out—Ben looked at me and saw the truth under all the layers that I hadn't been able to see myself.

But we don't get a chance to say anything more, because Chloe rushes into the room, her face flushed and panicky, waving a note in the air, trying to catch her breath to get out the words: "You got another letter."

50

JANEY

IN THE WAITING AREA, I squeeze Bill's arms and gather my things.

"I'll see you at home for dinner?" I ask him.

"Yeah. I'll spend some time with Ben, then I'll head home." He hesitates, watching me. Then he runs a finger slowly down my arm.

I flick my eyes up to his, questioning. His touch isn't sexual or possessive or intended to stall me. In his eyes, I just see wonder. A desire to touch me, still. Even after all these years.

My hair is as long and as wild as the day he met me. My tank top shows off my tanned shoulders and toned biceps. But that's not why he's touching me.

"You should talk to Ada," Bill says softly. "It might be a good time. She has a lot going on. It would be nice for her to hear it from you. About Ben...but also about the other stuff."

I hold his gaze.

It took a long time to be able to do so. To let him see me, beyond all the flounce.

"My flounce is what you fell in love with," I had complained to him once, when he hadn't stood for me avoiding his gaze, his words.

"No," he had corrected me, "that's what I fell in *lust* with. Lust can fade pretty quickly without something more substantial to ground it in."

Privately, I disagreed with this. I've known many men who could ride on the wave of lust for a very long time indeed. Men who didn't insist on delving a bit more deeply. At one time, I had imagined I would need to pander to their needs my entire life.

Then there was Bill. I can't imagine a better man anywhere in the world.

I still can't believe that I'm married to him.

So if Bill is asking, I pay attention.

I don't want to talk to Ada. About Ben, fine. I should have said something about that a long time ago. It always slipped my mind.

The other stuff, though. I really don't want to talk to Ada about that.

51

ADA

Chloe stands in the doorway.

Ben and I stare at her.

I had forgotten all about the letters.

For a minute, we're all suspended in this strange moment. Nobody moves. My thoughts struggle slowly to make a decision about what to think, let alone about what to do. Then I reach my hand out at the same time that Chloe starts talking.

"It went to the office. Casey let me know. She sent one of the interns to drop it to me out front."

It's another single page, the typewriter font with no signature.

Ada. If you won't reply, then I'm just going to have to come in person.

I hand it to Ben wordlessly. He skims over it, glancing at me. I shrug. I had given him the brief version—*Kingston can't be sending the letters. Turns out he died two years ago. I need to tell you something else about him, but not now.*

"I have no idea who this person is. Who sends three letters

without signing them? Or, for that matter, without leaving contact details? How do they expect me to reply?"

Though I'm deeply relieved that they aren't from Kingston, a whole new type of unease is settling over me. Firstly, that I have to tell Ben about Kingston. And secondly, that there's another unknown person out there who wants something from me, and I don't know what it is they want.

We're interrupted by a knock on the door.

"Lucas. Mate." Ben goes to sit up, and grimaces in pain.

"Jesus. You've really done a number on yourself, haven't you?" Lucas's gaze moves from Ben to me then Chloe. He grins. "Nice to see you've got some good company. How are you, Ada? Long time no see."

I smile at him. Lucas is good fun. "I've been better, Lucas. Too many crazy balls in the air at the moment."

We exchange news briefly, then I beckon Chloe out of the room. "We'll leave you two to catch up. Call if you need me," I add to Ben.

THE REST of the day passes between keeping Ben company, trying to get updates on when he can go home and what he'll need, and thinking about these letters.

Chloe goes home to Trevor with strict instructions for the office to contact her if any more letters arrive, or any strangers ask to see me.

Ben is still dozy, and though I'm desperate to talk to him more about what he said earlier, there's something soothing about sitting beside him, holding his hand. It feels like stolen time, where there is a reason—an excuse—not to talk to him about Kingston, mistakes, wasted time. Because whatever he says about loving me, I am not sure how he will react when he hears about just how wrong things really went.

Is it forgivable, I wonder? To not save someone who hurt you? Who was dangerous? I can forgive myself, sure. But will other people?

Will Ben?

When visiting hours are over, I tell Ben that I'm heading home and that I'll be back the next day. He looks alarmed.

"What about these letters? Is someone going with you?"

I pause. I had forgotten about them, again.

"Shit," I mutter.

"Call Lucas. He can take you home or take you to his place."

I squirm, thinking that it's overkill.

"But it's not Kingston. And I can't think of anyone else who'd want to hurt me. I can't work these stupid letters out. But I don't think I'm in danger."

"Bad luck," Ben says, eyeing me warily. Knowing he can't stop me if I just walk out, probably.

"Are you thinking about how you're going to make me when you can't even get out of bed?" I giggle, and he breaks into a smile.

"You will obey me," he says, raising his eyebrows with mock sternness. "Or I...will think up a punishment." His eyes wander down the length of me lazily, then come back up to meet mine. I feel a pulse start between my legs. The man only has to look at me...

"Come here," he whispers, and I move closer to the bed, already planning how to stop him, but he slides a hand laconically between my legs, under my skirt, stopping right at my crotch. His breathing is as heavy as mine.

Slowly, slowly, he slides his thumb along the outside of my underwear. His eyes don't leave mine.

"I want to smell you," he whispers, sliding two fingers inside the cotton, between my folds, finding my wetness, and he groans.

I feel like my knees might buckle.

"The nurses..." I murmur.

"Just for a minute," he mutters, pressing a finger inside me, his thumb finding my clit. "God, I want you to sit on my face right now. I want to lick you, or stick my cock into you, or something...delicious..."

"Ben," I mutter, knowing he should stop, thinking I must make him stop, but instead finding my legs moving a little wider of their own accord, giving him more room to explore me, to touch me. He groans again. "You want me to fuck you, don't you, Ada? You want to feel my cock, rubbing right here, pushing into you, parting your beautiful wet lips, while you lean over the bed, holding on to the sheets as each thrust...in here...nearly lifts you...off your feet...my hands...on your arse...thrusting...."

His thumb is frantically circling my clit, his fingers pushing in and out of me, and it's so hot, so illicit, so public that I cry out already, my orgasm hard and fast, his fingers pushing up deep inside me, my insides clutching at them like I want more, deeper, further. I lean over the bed, partly to steady myself against it, partly to kiss him, my tongue finding his, my need still overwhelming me. He's lying back, his eyes closed, his other hand coming around to grip the back of my head as he kisses me back. When I finally pull back he's smiling slightly. I rock against his fingers one more time, then he slides them out of me, bringing them to his lips.

"I've missed the taste of you," he murmurs, his eyes still closed. "I can't wait to lick you again. However you want it. If you want to never play a sex game again and do it missionary style for the rest of our lives, I'll still die the happiest man on the planet."

52

ADA

As it turned out, Ben didn't need to call Lucas to escort me home, because Bill texted.

Bill: *We're outside. Can we give you a lift home?*

Outside my apartment, I start to offer my thanks for the lift, when Bill asks if they can come in for a cup of tea.

"It's pretty late," I start to say, but Bill's eyes meet mine in the rearview mirror, and he gives a little nod. He's telling me to say yes, and I cringe on the inside. *Ben.* Oh God. Are we going to have the awkward conversation about Ben? Now?

But I agree, smiling graciously, and watch Bill take Mum's hand in the lift, stroke the back of it rhythmically. She looks fretful, which stands out on Janey. It doesn't suit her. My stomach lurches nervously. I wonder what she wants to say.

While I busy myself making tea, I can hear their low voices from my lounge room. It seems like Mum needs some encouragement. I hope Bill isn't coaching her to be supportive of Ben and me being together. I really don't want to have this conversation at all. Chloe said it's okay. I could leave it at that and skip the fanfare.

"Here you go," I murmur, handing them mugs of steaming

tea, glancing between the two of them, looking for a sign of what's to come. "I'll just get mine."

Back in the kitchen, I take a deep, steadying breath, then head back in, gripping my hot mug between my hands.

There's awkward silence for a while.

"So, Ben seems to be doing well," I venture, watching Bill for a reaction, wondering what I should do to speed them up. When no one says anything, I decide to just plunge right in.

"Chloe tells me that you know Ben and I have been together through the years?" I watch Mum carefully, making a question so she has to respond in some way. But she doesn't. She seems quite agitated. I press on: "I should have told you sooner. I thought you wouldn't approve."

At this, her eyes find mine. "Why do you care what I think, darling? You've always done whatever you liked. I'm surprised. I hope it hasn't been too difficult for you."

I want to throttle her a little bit.

I force myself to meet her eyes and speak calmly. "Yes, it has been, actually. Difficult."

She worries at the hem of her skirt, her fingers' constant movement at odds with her usual demeanour.

She glances at Bill, who nods encouragingly. Almost like one would a child.

"It's fine, darling. It's not like you're blood-related. We don't care, do we, honey?" This is directed at Bill, almost like a request for him to take over the conversation, take it out of her hands. It's odd to see my mother like this. Deferring to someone. At a loss for words. I look at Bill questioningly.

"I've had a chat with Ada, love. She knows I'm fine with it. And to hell with what anyone else thinks. As long as you two are happy."

Mum picks at a loose thread on the hem, her focus on it absolute. I wait.

Bill clears his throat. "Janey has something else she'd like to tell you," he says, still looking at her. His hand closes over her fidgeting one, encapsulating her fingers, the hem, the loose thread. He nods toward me. Mum looks petrified. I wonder what on earth she could have to tell me that has her in such a state.

"Well," she says, her eyes darting around the room. Anywhere but into mine. "It's about your father."

That surprises me.

I don't have very many memories of Dad. It wasn't that I was so young when he left—I must have been four or five. Chloe remembers more, but not much more. A present. A drive to the snow. Occurrences that stand out because they were so rare.

Mum rarely told us about him, and his photo was markedly absent from any collections in our house. I still don't know why they broke up. *'Oh, you know, we grew apart,'* was all she ever offered when I asked.

There was a period as teenagers where he'd call and speak to Chloe. More often than not, he'd not ask to talk to me. Sometimes Chloe would say: "Ada's here. Would you like to...?" After he'd hung up, she'd look at me apologetically. "Someone was at the door," she'd say, or "His train just arrived." I took it to mean he didn't care for me—but he'd never played a big role in my life anyway. After the first couple of times, I don't remember shedding any tears about it.

"Okay," I say, and wait some more. Bill is still holding Mum's hand, stroking it gently.

"He wasn't your father," she says eventually, her voice choked.

I reel back in surprise, slopping some tea over the edge of my mug. Luckily, this conversation is taking so long it's no longer scalding. My mind immediately starts freewheeling. Did she cheat on him, and that's why he left? When he found out I wasn't his? No wonder he never wanted to speak to me—

Bill gives me a look that is both gentle and a warning. It's a good thing he's here, or I might throw around some of these accusations out loud.

"I went to a concert when Chloe was little. He hated me going out. He thought I should be at home with Chloe. I thought he'd come round, come with me. I organised a babysitter. I got all dressed up. I hadn't been out, really out, since she was born. It was Elton John! It was magical." At this, her familiar enthusiasm lights up her face. "You should have seen—" But Bill cuts her off. "Darling," he says softly.

She slumps a little further into the sofa.

"I was raped," she says, her tone flat, her face blank. "There were four men. I was walking home by myself. They offered me a lift. I was young and carefree. I didn't think anything bad would happen. Then they drove me to a park and all had a turn with me."

My shock is absolute.

As much at her monotone as by the thirty-something years of silence.

For once, my eyes stay on her, rather than flitting to Bill for further understanding.

"I'm so sorry, Mum," I whisper, tears filling my eyes.

"Eric blamed me. He said I must have flirted. Led them on. He thought of me as soiled after that night. And when I found out I was pregnant, he couldn't accept not knowing if you were his or not. We tried for a few years to work things out between us, but eventually he just left one day. He didn't tell me where he was going. I didn't try to find him."

Mum's voice is still flat, emotionless. Bill is looking worried.

"Remember what Kathryn said," he urges her softly. "Why don't you tell Ada about how you felt?"

"I can't," she whispers, her face stricken.

"You can," he reassures her. "I'm right here with you. It'll help. I promise."

Bill glances over at me. "Kathryn is a counsellor we go to together. We've been going for a little while now." He glances back at Janey. "Can I tell Ada what we're working on?"

"Sure," she says, retreating behind her dull, flat voice again. Not looking at me.

"Kathryn thinks that your mum has buried some feelings so far away that she's never addressed them or worked through them...and so she shies away from any feelings, about anything. Which means she finds it hard to be connected to other people." He looks at me meaningfully. "So I'm hoping your mum can tell you a bit about how she felt at that time."

He nods at her encouragingly.

My head is spinning.

Mum looks at me. Her face remains blank.

"After Eric left, I had a paternity test done. I thought if you were his, he'd come back. That we'd work things out. But the test came back negative. I didn't know who your father was," she says, no emotion in her voice. "I didn't know who the men were. No charges were ever pressed. The police didn't take me very seriously. I had a bit of a reputation as a party girl. Even though that was long before I had a family. But I didn't love you any less —" Here her voice does crack, but she steadies herself and goes on.

"It's okay to cry," Bill murmurs to her, but she juts her chin out determinedly.

"Eric tried to love you too, at first. He really did. He was just eaten up with jealousy and anger. And there was no one for him to blame. So it kind of came to me. And when he left, Kathryn thinks I just shut down. It was all too painful. I had loved Eric so much and he didn't believe me—" And finally a sob escapes her. "And I was left with two little kids, and no money, and it wasn't my fault. No one cared. No one even asked if I was okay, after what those men did to me. And I just got on with things. I tried to be bright and happy for you girls, but I felt...numb. I didn't mean to. I just...stopped feeling anything. I kept everything superficial...everyone out...so I wouldn't get hurt again. Because Eric...he was the one person who was supposed to be on my side...and fight for me...and he didn't. He discarded me. I felt so worthless." Here again, Janey chokes up. Her shoulders shake silently as she tries to regain control of herself.

Bill holds her hand and rubs her back gently.

I can't think of anything to say—I'm too dumbfounded. Too choked up myself.

After a few minutes, Mum wipes her eyes and finally looks at me. "I wasn't really there for you and Chloe, growing up," she says. "I know that. Bill's helping me to try to do things differently. But...it's hard. I've never stopped to think about why I do the things I do. They just happen automatically. So it's easier to just carry on the way I always have. Not caring too much. Not getting involved in...feelings. Like if I let myself care..." Her voice trails off.

"I'm not going anywhere," Bill murmurs to her. He looks relieved. Like this has gone the way he hoped it would?

"We should let you get some sleep," Bill says, confirming this theory. "But I've been hoping Janey would tell you that for a while. I think it will really help you both...going forward. And now—well, we've just been talking about these letters. And..." He looks at Janey, and she looks straight at me again.

"Eric got in touch recently. He wanted to know about you and Chloe. And we just thought, tonight, I mean, we wondered....could he be sending you these letters?"

IT'S NOT until after Bill and Janey leave that the unlikelihood of that catches up with my shocked and sluggish brain. We'd agreed to talk about it the next day, because it was late, and I couldn't think properly after Mum's revelations. But as soon as they left, it was all I could think about.

Like—how would he know where I work? Where Chloe lives?

About Ben and me? And why would he write to me, and not Chloe?

And if he wanted to get in touch after so many years absent, I think a reasonable person would know that they'd need to sign off with their name and contact details. You might expect someone close to you to know your writing style. My father? Not so much.

I give up on my cold tea, tossing it down the sink, and pour myself a large glass of a local Shiraz, breathing in its heady, heavy scent and falling backwards into my sofa.

This evening. Yesterday. Friday.

Life has just crashed completely off course. Inexplicable, unpredictable. Completely out of control.

But as I lie there with my wine, closing my eyes between sips, letting thoughts roll over me without trying to beat them into some kind of order, I feel strangely relaxed.

Strangely okay.

53

BEN

DECEMBER 1, 2017

The doctor clicks his pen and tucks it into his white jacket.

"So just need to shit, huh, doc?" I smile at him.

He's told me that when I've been to the toilet, he'll discharge me. Provided there's someone with me for the first two weeks and that I put absolutely no weight on my leg until I'm given the all-clear. A nurse and a physio will visit me at home regularly to check on my incisions and to help me with exercises to build up strength and flexibility.

"Well, it's not just the bowel movement," he tells me, serious. "There is that. But also, I want to make sure you can manoeuvre yourself around a bathroom. Get up and down. We'll send you home with crutches, a shower chair, some dressings, and a few other tools to help you, but it's going to be tough. You're going to need help."

"I'll be there," Ada pipes up behind him, and my heart squeezes in my chest. "It'll give me an excuse to stay away from possible stalkers." She nods at me, her face blank, after he leaves.

"Right," I tell her. "It's for purely selfish reasons. I shouldn't feel special or anything."

"No way," she says, then breaks into a smile. I haven't seen her look so relaxed in a long time.

"Seriously, though—what about the magazine? You won't be able to help me and work 'til nine o'clock."

"Jase is going to step up," Ada tells me breezily, waving her hand around like her magazine, her favourite thing, the thing that has consumed her attention for a decade and a half, is nothing much. "He's been dying to get rid of me for a while. Too fastidious or something. And I'll be on call, if anything comes up."

I stare at her.

"You're going to go insane," I say, wondering if this is a terrible idea. The thought of having Ada all to myself for a week or two had seemed blissful when she first suggested it. But there is no way she's going to be calm and helpful while someone else runs her magazine.

She looks at me sheepishly. "I'm trying to adjust the rules. I have to practice as though the rule were true. You know, like—I will not die if the magazine is not run to my exact standards for a week or two. And even if a mistake creeps in, I *still* will not die."

"You're seeing your therapist again?"

"No," she says, irritated. "I haven't had time to see a therapist. Jeez. I've been fielding family crises and deep-and-meaningfuls left, right, and centre." Then she looks sheepish again. "I kept notes last time. I dug them out. They're very...thorough."

I laugh at that, and after an initial severe frown, the corners of her lips twitch too.

"I'm going to enjoy having you wait on me for a while," I tell her, suddenly feeling horny as all fuck. Imagining all the commands that I could issue while it's just the two of us, stuck in my apartment together.

"Don't look too excited," she tells me, leaning close. She smells so delicious, so unique, so sexy. I close my eyes and breathe her in. "Because, you're going to be kind of helpless, aren't you? I'm not sure you'll be in any position to issue orders. It might be, actually, that I just do whatever the hell I think is best."

My eyes fly open at her soft, seductive tone and meet hers, just inches away from me. Then she leans in and kisses me softly on the lips.

"You always have been very good at knowing what is best," I murmur, trying to capture her, deepen the kiss. But she pulls away from me, laughing.

"I need to go do a few last minute things in the office. I'll be here in the morning to pick you up."

As she walks away, she looks back over her shoulder and smiles at me. Something about it makes my chest tighten again. It's not sultry or flirty or teasing or playful. It's kind of...normal.

Just a woman smiling at her man. Who she gets to take home the next day.

54

ADA

Two weeks later—December 15, 2017

"Just until Wednesday. I promise."

"You don't have to promise anything," Jason replies, with a hint of wonder in his voice. "Take as long as you need. Hell, take 'til after Christmas. It's close enough."

"Nice try," I shoot back. "I know the final exec meeting is on Wednesday. Who knows what changes you'll try to sneak through if I'm not there? Probably everyone's already going home at 4 p.m. and having group cake-making sessions in frilly aprons in the meeting room twice a week."

Jason laughs. "How is the patient?"

"He's fine. Playing it up for all it's worth. Watching cricket and footy and eating pies. I don't think he wants to get better."

"And you? How are you coping with being away? Really?" His tone is serious. It's like I've migrated to Mars or something.

"Surprisingly well," I tell him, the subject having been at the forefront of my mind these last few days. "I'm cooking proper meals and baking slices. Don't get me wrong—I wouldn't want it to go on much longer. But once I decided to do it, it was actually okay. Enjoyable, even. Do you know, I can now make paella? I'm not sure I ever want to make it again. It took bloody forever. But nice to do once, I think. I feel like a real 60s housewife. Fascinating."

After we hang up, I wander back into the lounge room, where Ben is set up on the couch, surrounded by various remotes and DVD covers. He shoves some of them aside and pats the space beside him.

I sit obediently, snuggling under his arm.

"So...we never worked out those recent letters," he says, kissing my forehead. "Any thoughts about what to do about that?"

I feel strangely disinterested in the letters. For now, cocooned in Ben's apartment, testing the waters of domestic bliss, I've just put them aside to be dealt with later.

At their mention, though, the other unfinished complication springs to mind. I still haven't told Ben what happened with Kingston, that last time. It's hanging over me, heavy and awful and complicated.

But surprisingly, it's just that.

Not anything more. Not coming clean, telling the police what really happened. For two years, I've dragged around with me the constant knowledge that I need to tell the police what really happened on the pier. That I need to do the *right thing*. Put it all to rest. Face up to the consequences. And suddenly, all that matters is telling Ben.

I think I might be able to sit with not. Not doing the right thing. Being imperfect. Facing forwards, not backwards.

"Hmmm" is all I say to Ben. For now. I just want to play house for a few more days. Before I go back out into the real world.

———

LATER THAT NIGHT—ROLLING out homemade pastry, no less—I get a call from Chloe.

With the phone tucked under my ear, she rattles on about

Christmas. She wants to have it at her house. Just the family. No one is to bring anything. She wants to cook, clean, and be merry. Oh, and they've started the process to adopt.

When I hang up, I'm smiling to myself.

For once, the thought of a family function doesn't make my blood boil. A day with Mum and Chloe and nice food and booze.

I surprise myself—I actually think I detect a trace of enthusiasm.

"We're going to Chloe's for Christmas," I tell Ben. "She said she's doing everything. So I thought we could take the booze. I'm thinking lots of bubbles. Any requests?"

Ben smiles up at me, his shaggy hair uneven on one side, his eyes warm. "Just you," he murmurs. "As my date."

He reaches for my hand and tugs me down toward him, his lips finding mine, one hand coming around my neck, the other manoeuvring me until I'm straddling him, his cast leg sticking out awkwardly behind me. I can feel his cock pressing into my crotch.

"Have I mentioned how nice it is having you living with me?" he murmurs. "I've been thinking that you should move in."

"Hmmm. You know, once that plaster is off, I won't be so accommodating. You'll definitely need to cook. That shit gets boring, really quickly. I was actually on to something, only doing it once a month. And as for all this sex with you lying back and thinking of England...that will definitely have to stop. I like a bit more variety in my sex life."

Ben grins, nuzzling my neck. "I've noticed," he murmurs, biting me gently. I squirm on top of him, feel his cock twitch beneath me. He bites me again, laughing. "I could be a kept man. I've always dreamed of a lazier life. We could get a dog."

"In here?" I laugh. "No chance."

"I never think of England, by the way," he adds, reaching under my shirt, trailing his fingers down my stomach, which clenches in response. "I always think about you, Miss Cosgrove. You completely consume me. Even when you're not here."

He nibbles at my neck some more, tugging gently on my hair. "But it's better when you're here."

"Really," I murmur, leaning back and pulling my shirt over my head. "Tell me what you think about."

"Which time? Because I think of so many exciting things involving your body. If I tried to tell you about all of them, you'd have to take a year off work. And you'd definitely have to move in."

"Mmm hmm." I lean away from him, undoing my bra, letting it fall from my shoulders. He runs one hand lightly across my collarbone, tugging at one strap to pull it away from me, discarding it on the couch. "Pick one."

"Well. I've been thinking about you helping me in the shower. And we both get so wet...so you're completely naked...with water running all over you...dripping off your nipples...here..." He leans down, taking my nipple in his mouth, his tongue circling around it slowly, his teeth lightly grazing it, his eyes never leaving mine. I groan, my head dropping back, and his other arm tightens around my waist.

"Look at me," he commands, and I open my eyes, looking back at him, my eyelids heavy with lust and pleasure.

He leans back into the couch, his fingers tracing down my cleavage, between my breasts to my tummy, then slowly moving along the outside of my jeans.

"Take them off," he whispers, and I stand up, still looking at him, slowly undoing my button, my zip. Then I turn around and push them slowly down my legs, taking my underwear with them, leaning over so he can see my arse, my slit and folds.

"*Fuck,*" Ben hisses behind me.

When I've kicked them right off, I walk over to the dining table and pick up a chair, bringing it back and placing it right in front of him. Then I sit down with my butt at the edge of the chair, leaning back, my legs spread. Slowly I start to circle my clit.

"Tell me more about the shower," I say softly.

Ben is staring at my fingers, my pussy, his mouth slightly open.

"I'm sitting in the shower chair. My cock is rock hard. You've been rubbing it with something...slippery... You lean over...and your arse is right in front of me..."

My fingers start circling faster. I can feel my cum pooling at my entrance. I spread my lips open, use two fingers to smear it around myself. Ben fumbles with his own zip, wriggling his hips to free his cock, one hand grasping the shaft firmly, his eyes not leaving my vagina. Slowly he starts pumping his fist up and down.

"Oh God," he groans. "I want to lick you and fuck you and watch you all at once."

"The shower," I gasp. I'm close already. I want to come on my fingers, then have him sink his glorious cock inside me.

"And my leg is suddenly okay...and I stand and grip your hips...and you're still fumbling for the soap...I thrust into you...and you're so wet...and tight...and you cry out with pleasure... you're holding on to the taps...your arms out...your tits moving as I thrust...and—"

But I'm no longer listening, my orgasm pulsing through me, my head lolling back over the chair, as I push two fingers far up inside myself, moving them gently with the pulsing of my insides, my breathing heavy in my ears.

"Oh God," I hear Ben groan, but I feel too limp to look up, to move. My limbs feel gloriously heavy and satisfied. I just lie there, feeling fulfilled.

Eventually I hear Ben start to laugh.

I raise my head to look at him. He's looking down in dismay, then looks up at me, his eyes dancing.

"I need some tissues," he tells me, grinning. "Please?"

THE NEXT MORNING, Bill and Mum drop by with fresh pastries and hot coffee.

After her revelations about my father, I've tried to be less quick to judge her. Every time I try to imagine what she went through, I just end up in tears, it's so horrific. I can't actually imagine. My mind short-circuits, trying to comprehend it.

She seems more grounded, somehow. Like in speaking her truth, she can't hide behind false cheer anymore. And when she failed to engage with a topic last week, I felt compelled to bring her back to it, instead of stewing on it and her inadequacies. For both of us. I said 'This is important to me. I would really like you to listen and try to understand.' She actually sat down and took my hand and looked at me, serious. She was agitated, flighty...but she sat. And stayed.

Today, though, she gets straight to the point.

"I think I might have screwed up with something. About Eric. I might have told him where you work. And maybe...where Chloe lives. And possibly...that you were with Ben. I'm sorry," she rushes on, before I can speak. "I can't really remember. I'd had a glass of wine. His calling me was so infuriating. I don't really know what I said to him. I was furious. Like how dare he claim to give a shit *now*. Like he deserves to have you in his life *now*. Not when you needed him. Not when I needed him. And I think I was so angry that I wanted him to know that you were doing just fine without him. You had a good job. A great partner. That we didn't need him. So...it's actually feasible that he sent the letters. Maybe."

I ponder this. Mum looks worried that I'll be cross, but I don't really care. I've managed for thirty-seven years without my father. And the ripple effect of his not supporting Mum... well, I think I can manage another thirty-seven without him, too.

"Do you have contact details for him?" I ask her now. "Let's call him now. Let's just find out."

She shakes her head. "He didn't leave any. It was a private number."

Ben and Bill are both watching us. I roll my eyes in frustration. Who doesn't leave a phone number? Then I shrug. "If he calls again, ask. And you can tell him not to bother, on my account. I'm not interested in starting a relationship with him. He's thirty-three years too late."

Later, while we're watching *Notting Hill*, Ben strokes my hair and asks me if I really don't want to see what my dad wants.

"He's not my dad. Not biologically, and not in spirit. Bill is my dad, if anyone is. God, that sounds weird," I wince, glancing at Ben. "I still think it's a bit...something. I'm sorry. I'm going to get over it, I promise. But, we don't even know if it's him. Writing."

"It makes sense, though."

"Maybe." I'm silent for a while, thinking about the sudden changes in our family situation.

Ben shifts to face me, pausing the DVD.

"You haven't said anything about your biological father. How you were conceived. That must have felt big."

"You know, strangely, it hasn't. I feel like it should, but it just... doesn't."

I'm silent for a while.

"I think the thing that feels big is feeling some compassion for Mum. It doesn't change how she was. Or how it affected me. But now I get it. It's made me willing to try a bit harder. Especially because she's trying. I feel like...that deserves respect. She can't change the past. But at least she's been around, trying to be in my life, however superficially, for that thirty-seven years. Eric didn't even try. And maybe if I heard his story, I might have some compassion for him too. But right now, I just don't fucking want to."

"Fair enough. But you know, we'd never have met if he had

stayed. Sometimes I think, we all get dealt a hand. We all have to deal with things as they are. Maybe that's just the hand you got. Maybe that's what made you who you are today. And that's a pretty amazing woman. A beautiful, smart, funny, creative goddess, actually." Ben grins at me, pulling me in for a kiss, and I bat my eyelashes at him playfully.

God. How does this man manage to make every single difficult thing feel okay?

He looks serious for a moment. "You know, I'd like to wish you had a beautiful childhood, with two parents who saw who you were and loved you and you knew it. But then would we be here right now? Would you be the person that you are today, who I love so much? Sometimes I think it's helpful to remember that everything in your past has brought you to your present. Here, with me." He squeezes my hand and grins. "So maybe it was all really pretty fucking marvellous, actually."

Ben's hand is on my knee, his laughing eyes looking at me with his usual mix of ardour and adoration.

It's not perfect. It's not all clean and finished and sunny and nice.

I haven't told Ben about that night on the pier.

I haven't forgiven my mother, or worked out how to be with her in this new space. All I've worked out is that I want to try.

I haven't ticked everything off my list, efficient and orderly and neatly tied up.

But in a salute to everything I've learnt these last three weeks, I'm putting it aside.

I'm here right now, and it's pretty damn all right.

I'll tell Ben, and we'll work it out.

I won't tell the police, and I'll let go of the guilt and the shame. Or try to, at any rate.

I'll try to obsess about work a little less. Try to live by different, kinder rules. And fail sometimes. And survive the failure.

Chloe and Trev and Mum and Bill will be there next week, and the one after that. Infuriating and messy and annoying and mine. And they'll still love me, whether *Hot!* is one hundred percent perfect or only ninety-three.

And Ben. My lover. My partner.

Some people won't understand, will look at us strangely. And I'll learn not to care. Because this—messy and complicated and wonderful—this might just be everything.

So I smile and snuggle into Ben's chest.

And settle into my imperfect life.

EXCERPT - RUINED

A violent murder.
A family secret.
And a boyfriend who's not who he says he is...
Sydney, Australia. Lawyer and companion Natalie
Coommaraswamy struggles to be the good daughter her parents
demand. A second-generation Sri Lankan, she's never penetrated
her family's resolute silence surrounding their flight from Sri
Lanka, and has been left with unanswered questions about where
she belongs and who she can trust.
Then her best friend is found murdered. Fuelled by disinterest
from the police, Natalie begins her own hunt for the murderer.
But when clues point to her new lover, her carefully regulated
world starts to unravel. And the truth will threaten more than her
sanity...

PROLOGUE
Monday, March 26, 2018
The woman is well dressed, and the man is dead.

Her thousand-dollar Louboutins click on the marble floor as she makes her way out of the hotel room to the lift. She's unhurried; there's no one else on this floor, and the man made his own bed, so to speak. She has no qualms about leaving him lying in it.

In the lushly appointed bedroom, there's evidence of numerous lovers. Discarded high-quality bras and tiny g-strings in delicate lace, in varying sizes. Condom wrappers, champagne glasses, tousled bed sheets, and plenty of damp towels. It looks like an overindulgent orgy, starring the entitled git who's lying motionless on the lounge room floor.

White powder is carelessly cut on the glass coffee tabletop beside him. Bottles of champagne are half empty and going flat in various locations throughout the hotel room. The strong smell indicates at least some of it has been spilled sloppily on the luxurious carpet.

A silk tie hangs casually over a dining chair.

In the foyer, the woman glances without interest at the front desk, the security cameras, and the few people sitting in the hushed, plush interior. She walks out the three-metre revolving doors at the front of the building.

A few minutes later, she slips into a taxi. She pulls her long, black hair into a ponytail conspicuously, and looks the middle-aged driver in the eye.

She asks to be dropped off at a fancy café that she's never visited before, and pays with cash.

She doesn't give another thought to the dead man in the hotel room in Sydney's wealthy north shore. Rather, she enjoys her coffee, eggs, and smashed avocado without haste and without worry.

Then she goes home and gets on with her day.

Chapter 1

Five Months Earlier

Natalie cursorily flicks through yesterday's mail, then dumps it on her kitchen bench.

The marble bench top gleams brightly. Morning sun streams in the large window overlooking the empty street. The small lounge area is neat and clean.

Natalie feels a pang of guilt, which she quickly pushes aside, as she does every fortnight after the cleaner has been to her apartment.

The cleaner is the one luxury she affords herself. Three hours once a fortnight. She tidies, vacuums, and mops—all tasks that Natalie is perfectly capable of doing herself. Her apartment isn't even very big. She doubts it takes Mali three hours to clean it, but she hates the power imbalance between them. She hates another woman cleaning up after her. She pays her far more than the going rate to assuage her feelings on the matter.

Mostly, Natalie hates that she can still hear her mother's voice on the topic, even though she's never confessed to her mother that she has a cleaner—and even though she is thirty-eight years old, and it's frankly none of her mother's business. But frugality was drummed into her from a very early age. If you were to look in the third drawer under her gleaming marble bench top, you'd find neatly folded pieces of baking paper and aluminium foil, the faint outlines of biscuits or scones visible on them. Natalie can easily use them ten to fifteen times before needing to tear off a clean piece.

In her savings account, you'd find enough to comfortably pay a deposit on a second house in Sydney's north shores.

No one opens those drawers, though, or looks in her savings account.

Natalie has lived alone for seventeen years. As soon as she finished her law degree, she fled the family home, the relief washing over her from the moment she was handed keys to her very own space.

That same relief floods through her every time she arrives
back at her apartment after a family lunch, every second Sunday.

Now, however, she's still a week away from seeing her family,
and she pushes them out of her mind.

She kicks off her heels and runs her fingers through her
sweaty hair, collapsing on the couch, tilting her head back and
closing her eyes.

Her thoughts drift back to the problem.

The tiny, minute, yet very large problem growing inside her.

* * *

"You were at the gallery last night."

Natalie had startled.

*Her Uber had had a minor prang. While the driver had inspected
the damage, taken photos, and exchanged numbers and license
details with the other driver, Natalie had stood on the pavement, the
sunshine beckoning to her like a magnet. She was soaking it up, her
black hair getting hot under its rays, debating whether to walk the
rest of the way home to fully enjoy it, when a man had exited the
other car. He had waved dismissively at the driver, his phone glued
to his ear, indicating his watch and that he'd walk the rest of
the way.*

Then he'd seen Natalie and had stopped dead.

*She was dressed for work, her makeup flawless, her fitted red dress
showing off every curve. Its neckline was perfection—classy, but
showing just enough soft, tantalizing flesh that men always thought of
sex. A simple choker of pearls stood out around her neck.*

*Her appointment had cancelled and she was heading home, the
effort wasted.*

At least, wasted until this man was left staring at her, speechless.

*Natalie had cocked her head at him, watching. She had wished she
had a cigarette—inexplicably, she felt like blowing a waft of smoke
toward him. Not in his face. Just in his general direction. A challenge,*

maybe. A statement of independence, like she was a teenager playing truant from school, and what was he going to do about it?

It was such a clichéd moment. Hot man in suit notices sexy woman in dress.

Hot man stops and stares.

Except, in Natalie's line of work, this represented an opportunity rather than an inconvenience or an intrusion.

She wondered if the morning might not be wasted after all.

But then he had surprised her with the comment about the gallery.

He'd unceremoniously ended his call mid-sentence, as though the call was of no consequence whatsoever.

No consequence compared to her.

He fastened his dark eyes on her, and something inside her chest leapt erratically. Flashing danger signs glinted in his black eyes. For once, Natalie felt like the prey rather than the lioness.

He had stopped right in front of her, his broad shoulders and narrow hips clearly defined under his well-cut shirt. Not taking his eyes off her, he held out his hand. "Griffin," he said.

Natalie had taken his hand on automatic pilot. She felt mesmerized by his eyes. They were so dark. Framed with long, black lashes and beautiful pale skin, he looked half playboy, half wolf.

She shook his hand for a while before his half-raised eyebrow reminded her to speak. For some reason, she told him: "Ivy."

He kept hold of her hand. Emboldened by the effect he was obviously having on her, he kept it firmly in his, his thumb lightly running over her skin, his stare intense. He was thoroughly at ease in his own skin.

"You were staring at Jack Charles like you might somehow morph into him. You looked ethereal," he told her.

And somehow, all her rules had been broken.

Partly it might have been because you got the sense that people didn't say no to Griffin. Or maybe it was because he had noticed her at the art gallery—really noticed her. Not her curves, or her cheekbones, or her bewitching eyes. But her very being, in that moment, with that *picture. Which had spoken to her in ways that squeezed her heart, and bruised it.*

So she didn't quote him her rates. She didn't ask how long he'd like. She didn't play it for the cash. She let him take her to a hotel, and undress her, and command her, and marvel at her. She let him go down on her until she came. Really came, in the unhurried way that you can when there's no clock ticking, and the man between your legs acts like there's no place in the world he'd rather be.

She never had casual sex.

She never let herself get lost in the moment.

She never spoke to someone in the bedroom freely—unedited, unmasked.

She rarely spoke to anyone freely at all.

But Griffin was so intense, so attractive, so enamored by every inch of her, and had such presence, that she'd forgotten all the rules.

* * *

And now she was fucking pregnant. After twenty years of sexual activity so careful and pragmatic she hadn't had so much as a single itch that made her wonder if she needed an extra check up—one moment of unthinking passion, of using someone else's condom (*God, it must have broken. How old had it been? She had never had a breakage, in all her years of considerable sexual activity*), and all of that was out the window.

Then again, she doubted Griffin ever waited very long between conquests. It felt almost like a sign.

Despite this, she knew what needed to be done. She was not in any place to be a mother, even if she wanted children.

Which she didn't.

But somehow, Jack Charles's beautiful face, his story, Griffin's white-hot, insatiable desire, and her reasons for not wanting children were all tied up in a messy great ball that Natalie was in no mood to try to untangle.

She's interrupted by her mobile ringing, anyway.

"Can you come by a bit early on Sunday, Natalie?" Upeksha asks when Natalie answers the phone.

Natalie is used to the lack of preamble and pleasantries. It suits her well to get straight to the point.

For a while she had tried ignoring her mother's calls between Sunday lunches, feeling that the fortnightly interaction was quite enough family time. That only lasted until Upeksha sent a police car around to her apartment for a welfare check. The officer had peered around Natalie's door curiously.

"Your mother says you haven't answered the phone for two days." He left the statement hanging there.

Natalie had shrugged helplessly. "She fled civil war. She's always assuming the worst."

For some reason, when someone else raised their eyebrows judgementally at her mother's behavior—no matter how objectively crazy it might seem—Natalie's first impulse was violence. When it was just Natalie, deliberately letting the twelfth call go through to voicemail, her irritation and incredulity were unmatched by anyone. But the officer's slight sneer down his nose at her, his look of disbelief at the sparkling wedge of home he could see behind her, made her dig her fingernails into her palms so hard the resulting little half-moon indents in her skin could be seen for the next half an hour.

It was more than a desire to protect Upeksha. It was like a reverse mother's instinct, exacerbated; like a rabid dog. *Natalie* might be allowed to think Upeksha was completely bonkers. But this twenty-something white guy—who knew nothing of war and survival and assimilation—was most certainly not.

"Mmm," she answers her mother now, noncommittal. "What's up?"

"Your father has decided that you do so well on the stock market, that he'd like a lesson. We have some savings he'd like to trade with."

Inwardly, Natalie groans.

Her father will never trade a dollar on the stock market. Once she has shown him, in detail, how it works, he will at first think he is missing something. When it finally dawns on him the amount of risk involved, he will change his mind quick smart.

But it's no good trying to explain that to him; it's not fathomable to him that Natalie would risk her money in that way. If learning to trade is going to baffle him, learning how reckless his only daughter is with her money will baffle him even more.

Natalie agrees to help, though. Before Sunday rolls around, she'll have to come up with a way to avoid that particular lesson. Not least because she hasn't traded on the stock market for a good eight years.

Ironically, after getting her first big break from her first bad trade, she had bought her modest apartment in Sydney's middle-class South Coogee, and then had no cash left to trade with.

The lucky stock was one of her earliest purchases, before she had really learnt what she was doing. It immediately started heading downhill, and she had stubbornly refused to sell it at her stop loss, the idea of losing three-thousand dollars intolerable to her bank balance and her ego. Within a week it was at a quarter of its value. Fifteen-thousand dollars down, Natalie had never not honored a stop loss again.

But it was worth so little by then that she had forgotten about it for three years. Initially, she checked it hopefully every day, and it continued to bounce between two and four cents, a sad little line on her charts that was a painful reminder of her mistake. Her ego.

But then, routinely forgotten, her twenty-grand investment was "suddenly" worth three-hundred-thousand dollars, and Natalie was rich, by most people's standards.

Except it wasn't an investment. Natalie exclusively traded short-term, keeping stocks for less than thirty days, taking advantage of small fluctuations in the market, making only a few hundred dollars on every trade. But her three-year "mistake stock" had earned her the most money she had ever made in her entire life.

It was hard to keep remembering it was a mistake after that.

Natalie imagines her father's face. They'd sit down at the computer, his spectacles pushed to the rim of his nose, his legal pad and pen at the ready, a calculator by his elbow. He would expect Natalie to go through the process, and he'd take notes meticulously, expecting to be able to follow an A, B, C in a neat linear fashion—from the lesson to steady income once they had finished.

Ravi approached everything in life with due diligence. He combated whatever he had endured in Sri Lanka with order, patience, and as much Englishness as he could muster. Both her parents already spoke perfect English when they arrived in Australia—Ceylon being a British colony before regaining independence. But they had bought land in the whitest suburb in Sydney that they could afford. They had given their children the most Australian names they could come by. And they considered themselves as white as the next person.

Ravi would approach a lesson on the stock market in the same way. Learn the rules, play by them. At some point, he would carefully click the lid back onto his pen, and look at Natalie in a meaningful manner. He was an incredibly smart man. He would appreciate the complexities. But he would not appreciate his daughter taking such risks with her livelihood, day in, day out.

Risk and uncertainty were not part of Ravi and Upeksha's way.

Risk could lead to standing out from the crowd.

Drawing attention to yourself.

Being different.

It could lead to surprises and uncertain outcomes.

Not that Ravi would say anything. He would look at Natalie meaningfully and expect her to step back into line.

To be sensible. To contribute. To be valuable.

To not *risk* things.

Natalie needs to find a good way to dissuade Ravi about the merits of the stock market without going through that exhausting process.

She supposes she could tell him that she no longer trades—but her current profession is hardly going to be an improvement, in his eyes.

Eventually, she settles on telling him that due to the uncertainty around the Trump presidency, she feels the stock market is too volatile at the moment. She's gone back to law.

By the time she's solved this problem, she slumps on the couch, defeated.

She doesn't make an appointment to see her doctor.

Chapter 2

The man watches the woman carefully.

He knows her name, her height, her eye color.

He knows where she catches the bus into the city and where she frequently sees her clients.

He doesn't know what she sounds like when she laughs, or what type of wine she likes, or what she plans to be when she quits escorting in a few years' time.

He doesn't know about the homework club she volunteers at once a week to support teenagers with their learning—on the surface, or with their sense of belonging—a deeper, and more important goal.

He does know what she'll look like with his hands around her throat, though.

He's seen how that looks several times before.

Chapter 3

By the time Sunday lunch rolls around, Natalie still has not made an appointment to see her doctor.

She feels decidedly queasy as she drives the thirty minutes to her parent's house in Linfield—the same house that she grew up in, that houses all her childhood memories. Occasionally, one jumps out at her, wraps her in its thick, tight, suffocating grasp— but mostly, she tries her damnedest to keep them in the past, where they belong.

Alex opens the door for her, his smile wide.

"Natty!" he cackles excitedly, reaching forward to hug her, his delight infectious. "I've missed you! I've missed you! What has kept you gone so long!" It isn't a question, more a statement of his excitement that she's here now. The conversation goes much the same way every second Sunday.

"Come," he beckons her, already heading toward the stairs leading up from the foyer to the bedrooms.

A place, Natalie knows, where it's harder to keep bad memories at bay.

"Let me say hi to Mum and Dad," Natalie says gently, nodding at him encouragingly, but a dark cloud passes across his face.

"Now! Now! Now!" he repeats, jabbing his finger toward the top of the stairs, the volume increasing with each word and each jab. Natalie sighs, and acquiesces.

His bedroom looks much the same as when Natalie left home, though he's two years older than her. Figurines of various superheroes are littered across the bed and floor. The bookshelves are lined with comic books and adventure stories. Terry Pratchett simpers from a poster above the bed.

Generally, Natalie's parents don't like her to go into Alex's bedroom without one of them present, but she has never felt afraid of her brother. He seems as manipulable as a child.

"New—see?" he says, pointing at a figurine that Natalie doesn't recognize. It stands about twenty centimeters high and has the bright, waxy look of something not yet well-handled, not worn down by hours of attention from small, grubby hands.

Except Alex's hands are not small. At six feet, he towers over Natalie, the disparity between his body and his mind as painful to her now as it is every time.

"Lovely, Alex," she tells him softly. "Tell me about him."

Alex bounces on the balls of his feet happily, recounting something about Wolverine's powers. Natalie nods encouragingly, keeping eye contact, wistfully grateful that she is able to provide this small slice of comfort in his day. His little sister—interested, warm, attentive.

He's joyful about the smallest things.

Every time Natalie sees him, her heart breaks in two all over again.

* * *

Upeksha has made enough roast to feed twelve people.

The four of them sit around the formal dining table, Alex being reminded constantly to stay at the table until he has finished his meal and excused himself.

They make stilted small talk. As always, Natalie asks after Aunty She and Uncle Pu in Melbourne, her cousins dotted around Australia. Her mother gives tight-lipped replies.

Natalie keeps in touch with these extended family members herself, of course. She doesn't know why she provokes her mother so. It's almost like she's trying to demonstrate family solidarity, draw her mother back to her heritage, her country of origin, despite knowing perfectly well that Upeksha wants nothing less. Her sister and her family epitomize all the things that Upeksha and Ravi disavowed when they fled to Australia; they celebrate their skin color. They are at home in it. They visit Sri Lanka; cook curried mutton, pickle their own fruits, and make coconut relish.

The very opposite of assimilating.

But Natalie can't let it go. She couldn't let it go twenty years ago, and she can't let it go now.

"I went to the gallery to see the Archibald exhibition a few weeks ago," she tells her family. Jack Charles is still haunting her. The portrait of the Aboriginal actor and elder by Anh Do went on to win the People's Choice Award, and Natalie can't reconcile that with the people that she experiences in her life. That they would vote for a portrait of an Aboriginal man. A stolen man. An addict. *Which people voted for his portrait?* she wonders. Submitted by a Vietnamese-born artist, no less. A refugee, surviving five days in a leaky fishing boat, attacked by two different bands of pirates on his way here.

He'd be left to rot on Manus Island if he tried to come now, Natalie thinks to herself. The thought is unbelievable, unbearable. All the things Do has contributed. What things might those languishing on Manus Island have contributed, if they'd been given a chance?

Perhaps the artistic community are different, though, Natalie thinks. *Perhaps people who care about art are slightly more evolved, more refined, carry a softness or a sensitivity that is missing on the streets*. A whole other world to the people that Natalie encounters every day. The ones who slow their cars to shout obscenities to her out the window. The ones who watch her extra carefully in David Jones.

"I liked the portrait of Jack Charles. Did you see it won the People's Choice Award?"

Natalie knows that her parents would know this. Part of being white is keeping up with the culture. Art. Literature. They would have seen Jack's face. They would have passed over it hurriedly. Moved on to more European-inspired images. Traditional.

White.

"We preferred the one of Eileene Kramer," Upeksha says, without missing a beat. "So much beauty. So much stillness. And my, what an accomplished woman at 101! Imagine that. Still working. Still travelling. Still following her passions. Can you imagine being so immersed in something that you love, that you just never retire? I guess it's like football stars. They go on to coach, to be involved in the club in other ways..."

Natalie lets the words drift over her. She knows this dance well enough by now. Her mother beats back Natalie's mutiny by sheer volume of words. She drowns Natalie in them, suffocates her subtle rebellion in a tedious snowball of white words. The football, the cricket, the current issues of being Australian. After all these years, Natalie still feels a pang of heartache at the zeal with which her mother took on anything that she considered a commitment to their new life in Australia.

Usually, it was concurrently a nail in the coffin of anything to do with Sri Lanka.

It's always this way with her family.

A constant push-pull of longing for connection to her heritage—and her parents—and finding none. Natalie longs to hear stories of where they came from, even now. Even after thirty-odd years of being deflected or outright ignored. She wants to hear the good ones and the happy ones and even the hard ones. Especially the hard ones, perhaps. The ones that will make her weep, and despair, and fold into herself.

Her longing to know every little piece of who her parents were and what Sri Lanka was like for them is like an obsession.

To her parents, it is inconvenient at best and blasphemous at worst.

"It's not relevant," they say. "It's not important. Let's be grateful for what we have here," they tell her.

Deflect, deflect, ignore.

By the time they've had a cup of tea, Natalie is exhausted.

Alex is long gone, and she can hear him banging and shouting upstairs, his figurines fighting over imagined injustices, saving the day.

Where were they for you? Natalie thinks to herself. *Where were your heroes that day?*

She knows the answer though. They were busy pretending none of it was happening.

They were busy pretending to be white.

* * *

It's after 11 p.m. when she gets home.

She's already discarded her wig, her scalp warm and itchy from the extra layer and the weight of the thing. But her short, aggressive style didn't only horrify her mother.

To be fair, Upeksha had done everything she could to raise Natalie in a way to facilitate her fitting in. To help her to be invisible, or at least, only visible in the right ways.

Feminine ways.

Soft ways.

Ways that didn't make any trouble.

She thought that she was doing the right thing by Natalie.

But Natalie was none of those things. She was opinionated. With rough edges and strong features. She did not fade into the background. She wore her brownness like a talisman, as though in it she might belong, though the true meaning of the word was stifled underneath the way her parents attempted that very thing. Because fitting in for them meant safety and acceptance—life, even.

Natalie understood that. But she wished more than anything she could understand it in her bones. Know her parents' stories, feel them in her skin, have them as protection, as armor. Stories of survival, or heartbreak, or terror, or tragedy. Something she could belong to, whatever it was.

Because what her mother failed to understand was that being brown *did* make her different. Not to everyone. But to the kids at school who turned their noses up at her; to the parents who pulled their children away from her on the bus; to the grown men who shouted insults from their cars—Natalie *was* brown. And they rejected her.

So growing up, Natalie had found she did not belong anywhere. To her parents, the only acceptable daughter—the only *loveable* daughter—was one who was following their lead and living white. And to the white people she encountered in the schoolyard, on the bus—it didn't matter how hard she tried. She would never be white.

She was brown, and they made sure she didn't forget it.

Still, she thinks to herself now, perhaps she would grow her hair again. Though she loves it short—she feels more herself than she ever has—she hates the wig. And her bookings—and thus her income—dropped dramatically along with her long locks.

Yes, she thinks to herself. She'll grow it again, just while she's escorting. When she quits, she can always cut it off again.

She's just flicking through Netflix for something trashy and light to entertain her for half an hour when her phone pings.

Unknown: Ivy. I need to see you. Be ready tomorrow at 11. I'll pick you up. What's your address?

Natalie stares at the message, bewildered for a moment. Her work name on her private number. It makes no sense.

Then she remembers giving Griffin her number as he left. She didn't actually expect him to call, and rattled it off without much thought.

She gazes at her phone vacantly for a while.

As it happens, she has a booking tomorrow at 11 a.m. That aside, she doesn't like being told what to do.

And besides which—her line of work doesn't really lend itself to satisfying relationships. At least, that's what she tells herself as she deletes Griffin's message.

Then she books an appointment with her GP online.

Praise for Ruined

"LIANE MORIARTY, BUT GRITTIER." - *Catherine Deveny, Writer, Comedian, Author and Speaker*

"Mind-opening...Fascinating, frightening, very deep. Learned a great deal about human nature, suffering, and redemption... These characters are so real to me. An unforgettable, compassionate account. Many thanks to this author for tackling extremely difficult family dynamics, and for doing it so well!" ★★★★★ *Apple books review*

"What a thrilling story, with so much thought going in to every sentence. A very sensitive subject matter, but superbly written. It really grips you from the very first page. I highly recommend this book, you won't be able to put it down." ★★★★ *Amazon review*

"...fast moving and intriguing. A surprise ending. I recommend reading." ★★★★ *Amazon review*

"Wow! This book was not what I expected. It was extremely fast paced and dealt with many provocative subjects. Natalie, the main character, is very strong and I was pulled into her struggle instantly. This is a very thought-provoking, compelling, and complex thriller." ★★★★ *Amazon review*

"This is a story that will stay with me for a long time." ★★★★ *Amazon review*

"I am in awe of this writer and this story. It was so gritty and emotional and so compelling. I couldn't put it down. The emotions that ran thru and the intrigue kept you guessing...I don't say this often, this is a story not to be missed." ★★★★★ *Amazon review*

"This complex story took me by surprise. It is like nothing I have ever read. The characters are well written and developed. They are realistic and captivating. All of them had secrets...this is a book not to be overlooked. It is a must read." ★★★★★ *Amazon review*

"This story is brilliantly written and really grips you, keeping you guessing until the very end. I can usually tell how it will end or whodunnit but this time no matter how convinced I was about who it was, I was wrong and I love that!" ★★★★★ *Goodreads review*

"It's thrilling, a little scary, and intriguing...Hint: Your first, second, and third guesses are all wrong." ★★★★★ *Amazon review*

"This book was impossible to put down. Its a total page turner – intelligent, well-written and thoughtful content, intriguing story and topical themes. Highly recommend." ★★★★★ *Amazon review*

PLEASE NOTE: *This book is published without the steamy scenes as 'The Good Daughter". Please see my website for how to access the steamy version!*

ABOUT THE AUTHOR

S.A. McEwen writes nuanced and gritty psychological/domestic thrillers and romantic suspense exploring relationships, especially within families...with a particular interest in how the dark gets in, and the complex things that drive us toward or keep us out of connection with each other

She is a qualified social worker and educator in youth mental health, and lives in Melbourne with two gorgeous boys and a puppy.

If you've enjoyed her writing, please get in touch and say hello! The links are listed below.

Get notified when I **release a new book** via my newsletter here: www.samcewen.com.

f facebook.com/authorsamcewen

a amazon.com/author/samcewen

BB bookbub.com/authors/s-a-mcewen

g goodreads.com/samcewen

patreon.com/samcewen

ACKNOWLEDGMENTS

A huge thank you to my wonderful friends, Sarah and Steph, for reading the first draft and being enthusiastic, delightful, and hilarious commentators—again!

To my beta readers, Cat Skinner and Victoria Colotta—thank you for your thoroughness, your thoughtfulness, and your honesty. I really appreciated your feedback and your enthusiasm about this book.

To Alessandra Torre's Inkers—thank you. Thank you, thank you, thank you. I lurk quietly, but I love how much knowledge is shared so readily in our group.

To Erica Russikoff from Erica Edits for your amazing editing. I feel so confident sending my book babies on to you.

To Elizabeth Mackey for updating my covers for this series so beautifully.

And lastly and mostly to my husband—your supportiveness is beyond belief.

And to all of you reading this book—thank you for taking an interest in it. I really appreciate it, and I hope that you loved it as much as I loved writing it. x